So Long,

Lollipops

AN
Until the End of the World
Novella

Sarah Lyons Fleming

For the readers who let me know *Until the End of the World* meant something to them. Your words meant a whole lot to me.

And for my parents, who fully support my craziness.

CHAPTER 1

It wasn't the brightest idea to watch the pickup drive off, not with all the zombies at the foot of the dumpsters he stood on. But Peter knew he was going to die. And since he had only hours—or minutes—to live, he wanted to spend those last moments happy. Well, as happy as you could be surrounded by zombies.

But he *was* happy, which was mind-boggling, especially when you considered that he'd spent more than half of his life unhappy. He'd spent the last eighteen of his thirty years miserable, in fact, until he'd been saved. And now, as he watched the people who'd saved him jump the curb and swing out of the parking lot, there was happiness in the knowledge that he'd saved them back.

The minute John had pulled them behind the dumpsters and out of view of the Lexers in the alley, he'd known: either none of them would escape or all but one of them could. Bits sat between Penny and Ana, face pale, blue eyes frantic. She'd looked at him like he had the answers—the way a little girl looks at the daddy she believes will never let her down.

And although he supposed he'd already known, in that moment he realized he was the closest thing Bits had to a dad. He'd held her hand during the nightmares that plagued her. He'd cuddled her and teased her and named all of her freckles. And he loved her so much that when he imagined losing her it felt like looking into a black hole. Isn't that what black holes did—suck all light out of the space around them? That's exactly what would happen if Bits was gone.

He knew Cassie understood; if he was Bits's dad, then Cassie was her mom. He needn't worry as long as Bits was with her.

It had made the decision easy. Maybe once—a few months ago, even—he would have weighed his life against another's. Calculated pros and cons. Made a deal. He was good at deals. He'd spent years making them; he'd learned all about them at Harvard Business School. But there was nothing here to negotiate. It was refreshing. He was flooded with a resolve so strong, so sure and clear, that it was painless.

He didn't regret it, even as the torn, rotten hands scrabbled inches away from his boots. The racket they kicked up brought more down the alley. The Lexers on the other side of the fence, the one everyone had escaped over, struggled against the chain link now that his family was gone.

It may have made the decision easy, but he was still scared. He was really fucking scared. The hilt of his machete was slippery with sweat. He considered putting his gloves back on, but what was the point? He moved forward and drove his blade into the middle of a face. Another one down. There were so many, though. And they would keep coming, no matter how many he finished off. He couldn't win; it was all a matter of how long he wanted to live.

There was no way he was going to let them take him. He already knew that when the time came—when he was too tired to stand, or they got too close, or some tall basketball-player zombie was able to reach across the dumpster and get a grip on his ankle—he'd finish himself off with a bullet in the mouth. If there were any brains left in his head, he might become one of them, and that was not going to happen.

The dumpsters gave him a platform that measured around six by seven. Behind him was the brick wall of the building, and the other sides—well, those were all zombie. He drove the machete into a neck, then an ear. All that trench digging and wood chopping had made his arms feel tireless; he could do this for hours. So he would. He would fight until all he had was enough strength to pull the trigger on his last bullet—the one meant for him. He laughed, not that it was funny. Maybe he was losing his mind.

"Can't really blame me," he said to the hissing mass. "Can you, you stupid fucks?"

Cursing was good. Cursing made you angry. Anger gave you more strength. The machete flicked out again as he bent forward. The alley echoed with groans and filled with the smell of decay.

Actually, if he kept killing them, they might pile up and become a convenient staircase that allowed the ones behind to reach him. But the only other option was to watch them until he couldn't take it anymore, and then blow his brains out. Every Lexer he killed was one less monster in the world, one less threat to Bits, so he dismissed the thought.

There was an old lady at the far end of the dumpster. Her wrinkles had become deep cracks, and the tissue that peeked out, the tissue that should have been pink, was gray and veined with black. She reminded him of his grandmother, who'd been such a bitch. After Mom and Dad and Jane had died, she'd raised him in much the same way she'd raised Dad. And, if the fact that Dad had limited them to an annual visit was any indication, she hadn't been a candidate for Mother of the Year.

"They're gone, Peter," she'd say. "No sense talking about it."

So he'd learned to keep his mouth shut. But one day he'd tried to bring up how he knew that Jane hadn't died immediately in the crash, how he knew she'd been trapped in the fire. How every night in his dreams he watched her die, saw her begging for him to help her, to open her seatbelt. Just one little click, and she'd be free. He hadn't been in the car because he hadn't wanted to go, hadn't wanted to hang out with his nine year-old sister somewhere his twelve year-old friends might see. Or worse, be seen by a twelve year-old *girl*.

He needed someone to tell him it wasn't his fault.

Grandma cut him off. "You made a decision, Peter. Choices have consequences."

He'd taken those words to heart. He'd wanted absolution, but instead he'd gotten agreement.

Two steps down the seam where the dumpsters met, and the old lady was finished off. *How about that decision, Grandma?* It felt great. Years of therapy in one machete move.

"Hey! Up here!" a voice shouted.

Okay, now he was going crazy. He was even hearing voices. Real voices, not groans and hisses.

"Up here! Look up!"

There it was again. High-pitched and carrying over the Lexers' low noises. He should look up, just in case he wasn't going insane. If it was nothing, then he'd go back to killing as many Lexers as possible before that bullet. He pressed against the wall, as far out of their reach as he could, and looked up. There was a face looking down from the second story window. It was hard to tell from his vantage point, but it looked like a teenage girl.

"I'm throwing down a ladder!" she yelled. "Hold on!"

This wasn't part of the plan. Not that it wasn't a welcome change; as plans go, his had really sucked.

She reappeared and yelled, "Watch out!"

Peter caught a flash of short blond hair as she hooked a fire escape ladder to the windowsill and released the bottom. The chains that held the metal rungs clattered and rang. The dumpsters raised him a good five feet off the ground, and the bottom rungs hit them with a hollow bang. Peter watched in astonishment. It was unbelievable that he was being rescued from what had been a hopeless situation.

The blond head leaned out. "It's secure!"

A hand on his boot woke him from his stupor, and he swung his machete through the bones of the wrist and shook off the amputated hand. He slung his machete over his shoulder and reached for his daypack against the wall. The ladder swung as he climbed to the window, and the chorus of moans reached a crescendo, almost as though they were complaining.

He risked a downward glance and muttered, "So long, lollipops."

He planted his boot on the window ledge, and then he was in a small office. The girl stood close to the door, past two desks and a few file cabinets. She was about sixteen. Chin-length blond hair. A tiny nose. Wide eyes and rosebud lips. She looked like a little pixie. She smiled, but the pistol she was pointing at him was dead serious.

"*So long, lollipops?*" she asked with a cocked head. "*That's* what you say to zombies?"

Peter watched the gun and thought about his answer. She might be tiny, but she looked like she knew her way around a weapon. "I say that with my...little girl. Instead of *So long, suckers.*"

"That little girl who went over the fence? That's your daughter?"

"Sort of."

"So long, lollipops," she said again. A little giggle escaped. "I like it. So, I'm thinking you're a good guy, since you basically, like, volunteered to die for your friends. But I want you to take off your weapons anyway."

Peter pulled the gun out of its holster and slowly lowered it to the desk. Then he laid down his machete and stepped back. "I'm Peter. Peter Spencer."

She didn't seem particularly afraid, but he thought introducing himself might break the ice. Or at least get that gun pointing in a different direction.

She nodded. "Natalie. Nat."

"Thanks, Nat. For sending the ladder down. We didn't know there was anyone in the building."

He smiled; she flashed tiny white teeth in return. "Yeah, well, I couldn't just let you die after that whole martyr thing. Even though my dad and uncle are going to kill me."

"Are they here?"

"No, they went for supplies. They're fixing a place up. We're here for now, 'cause it's high."

She still had her finger on the trigger, although the pistol had fallen by her side. She screwed her mouth to the side and studied him. "So, Peter, you're not going to rape me or anything, are you?"

"No!" God, this crazy world, where a kid had to ask things like that. He opened his mouth again, but that was the only answer he had.

"I didn't think so," Natalie said. She waved her gun and shrugged. "But I figured it wouldn't hurt to ask. Grab your stuff. Let's get up to the third floor."

She led him into a hall lined with ugly brown carpeting. Footsteps carried up from the restaurant below. All those Lexers were still in the building. And they'd probably be there forever, since they were too stupid to find their way back out through the door they'd broken down.

Natalie opened a door to a narrow staircase and motioned for him to follow. Peter thought that she was far too trusting to keep her back to him, to take him only at his word. He wanted to tell her that, but this was one of those times when it was better to keep your mouth shut. The wooden stairs deposited them in the center of an open space that ran the length of the building. Two beds took up one corner, with a third across the room. The bright comforter and stack of young adult books by the lone bed were dead giveaways as to whose it was, although Peter remembered being a teenager well enough to not need those hints. No way would you want to sleep near your dad and uncle. Not if you were safe, anyway.

There was a sofa and coffee table. A table and chairs by the street-facing windows. A folding table and shelving unit held a camping stove, boxes and cans of food, assorted pots and jugs of water.

At the edge of the table was a handheld radio. The voice blasting out of it was deep and anxious. "Nat. Natalie! Are you okay? Answer me, damn it."

Nat skipped over to the radio. "Sorry, Daddy. I was on the second floor."

"Rich and I can see the group from here. What's going on?" His voice was less frantic now, although still concerned.

Natalie sat on a chair and crossed her legs. Her foot swung, like she was on the phone with a friend. "There were people down below. The zombies came in after them."

"What happened to them? Could you tell?"

Nat cut her eyes to Peter. "They got away, out the back. But one of them got stuck here." Her voice got higher, like a little girl. "Daddy, promise you won't be mad when I tell you something?"

"Spit it out, Nat."

"I kind of threw down the ladder and he's up here with me."

"*He's* up there? Natalie, what the hell?" He seemed about to go into a lecture, but then sighed. "Put him on. Now."

Nat held the radio out to him with a small smile. *She* might not be afraid of her dad, but Peter knew he should be.

"Hello?" Peter said.

"What's your name?"

"Peter. Peter Spencer."

"Peter, we're going to draw enough of them away to get up there, and I swear to Christ, if my daughter is harmed in any way, we will kill you. Understand?"

Natalie rolled her eyes and whispered, "Just say, 'Yes, sir.'"

"Yes, sir," Peter said. His life had taken many strange turns these last months, but for some reason, being threatened via radio by the father of the teenage girl who'd saved his life took the cake. "I wouldn't harm her. She saved my life."

"You'd better not. Give the radio back to Nat."

"Hey, Daddy," she said. "So, what's the plan?"

Peter had been thinking that she was altogether too lighthearted about this situation, both with him being a stranger and the fact that there were hundreds of Lexers downstairs, but now her posture straightened.

"Rich'll draw them away and swing back when he's far enough. I'll be there in a few. Sit tight."

"Okay."

Peter followed her to a window and watched a truck roll down the street. It was a big pickup, with an American flag decal across the rear window and chrome rims. It stopped just past the bar, windows lowered, and the music began. Not the music Peter would have ever guessed would come out of this truck. He'd been expecting classic rock or country-western, anything but the classical music that echoed off the cement and brick buildings.

He knew the piece. Grandma not only made him take dancing lessons, but she'd also expected him to go to museums and the symphony. It was Verdi's Requiem. And whatever orchestra was playing the piece was playing the hell out of it. The timpani crashed, the strings wailed, and the choir gave it their all. *Deliver me, Lord, from eternal death*—Peter remembered that one line from the end. If was a fitting selection.

The Lexers in the bar streamed out to meet the music. When they'd almost surrounded the truck, it pulled forward another half a block and stopped. It did it again and again, until a trail of zombies a block long followed it around the corner and out of sight.

"My Uncle Rich calls himself The Pied Piper of Bennington," Nat said.

Another truck pulled onto the sidewalk. Peter could make out a large-framed figure before it disappeared into the building. Footsteps thundered up the stairs. Peter quickly removed his gun, set it down on the table and stepped away from Natalie.

The man burst in. Natalie walked forward and wrapped her arms around him. "Daddy, this is Peter. I'm sorry, I know you say not to get involved, but he was going to die because he—"

The man held up the hand that wasn't holding a pistol. There was nothing about him that resembled his tiny elf of a daughter. He had a square face, ruddy cheeks and short brown hair with a beard. The only thing remarkable about him were his eyes, which were ice blue and, Peter guessed, probably friendly when he wasn't staring you down.

He raised his chin. "Let me hear what he has to say."

That was kind of open-ended. What should he say? What was most important? Probably that he didn't plan on sticking around and using up any of their valuable supplies. "We were on our way up to the Vermont Safe Zone. Kingdom Come. We got trapped downstairs, and I stayed behind so my friends could get out. I'd be dead if it wasn't for your daughter. I just want to continue on my way up there."

The man took off his flannel jacket to reveal a barrel chest and another large pistol. He waved his gun toward the door. "Well, get going then. Glad—"

"Daddy!" Natalie yelled. She stamped her foot. "You know they're still in back. Some of them are probably down the street. Peter has a little girl. She was one of the ones that got away because of him. You can't just send him out there!"

The man breathed in through flared nostrils. "That true?"

Peter nodded and held his breath. He didn't necessarily want to be where he wasn't welcome, but without a vehicle he might be dead in minutes on the street. The man lowered his weapon and looked at Natalie.

"You always say I'm a good judge of character," Natalie said. Her eyes widened and grew wet. "I saw the whole thing. He sacrificed himself for them. He was going to die! Daddy, you would do that for me, too."

Her dad's face softened. She was playing him, the same way Bits played Peter when she wanted an extra treat or another chapter. Not that what Nat was saying wasn't true, but it meant that she could accomplish in minutes what would take Peter days to do, in terms of gaining her father's trust. He couldn't resist Bits when her eyes were big and her lips trembled. The funniest part was that he didn't even mind he was being suckered.

"Take his weapons," her dad said, and Nat scrambled to grab his pistol and machete off the table. When her back was to her dad, she winked at him. This kid was bananas, as Nel would say.

"I'm Chuck," the man said. He holstered his weapon and extended a hand. The calluses were filled with dirt and grease. "We're going to hold on to those for now. This afternoon I'll see about helping you get a way out of here."

Peter realized his own hand wasn't much different from Chuck's. Chuck seemed to notice the signs of hard work and gave him a nod that, if not friendly, was respectful. "I'd appreciate that, Chuck."

"You might as well make yourself comfortable. Not much to do until Rich gets back."

Peter stripped down to his t-shirt and sat at the table. Natalie sat opposite and waved a magazine at her face. It was hot up here. And he had to pee. It was getting pretty imperative that he find the bathroom.

"Chuck," he said. The man looked up from where he was loading his pistols. Peter was pretty sure they'd already been loaded and that this show was just for him. "I need to use the bathroom. Where should I—"

"I'll take him," Nat offered. She leapt out of her chair and waved Peter up.

Chuck pointed her back to her seat. "No, I will."

He led Peter to the second floor and opened a door at the end of the landing. Peter realized they'd entered the second floor of the building next door. It was an apartment almost barren of furniture, probably where they'd gotten the stuff in their space upstairs. Peter opened the door Chuck had pointed out to find an actual bathroom.

"Looks right, but take a closer look," Chuck said. Peter walked to the toilet and opened the lid. They'd bored a large hole in the toilet's bottom and placed it over a hole in the floor. Anything and everything was being deposited into the dark of the floor below. It didn't smell great, of course, but it was pretty ingenious.

"We opened the windows down there, so there's no gas buildup. Don't want to blow ourselves to hell," Chuck said. "Well, I'll be outside."

When Peter came out Chuck was standing at the windows. "Sorry about your little girl. But I'm glad she's okay," he said, without turning.

Peter cleared his throat. "She's not really my daughter. I wish she was, but she's not." He didn't know why he felt the need to explain; it's not like Chuck was demanding a birth certificate.

Chuck turned and smiled. Peter had been right—those blue eyes were friendly when they weren't entertaining the idea of your demise. "Doesn't really matter, does it? Once they got hold of your heart, they got you. C'mon, let's head up."

***

Natalie had been grilling Peter for two hours by the time Uncle Rich's truck pulled up outside. Chuck had listened, asking the occasional question and nodding along when Peter described Cassie's cabin and the past few months.

The door opened, and a younger version of Chuck appeared, only with blond hair instead of brown. He skated his eyes to Peter and then back to his brother. "We good?"

Chuck nodded, and Rich walked over with a hand out, saying only, "Rich." To which Peter replied, "Peter."

Rich sat on the couch and drank from a bottle of water, then wiped his mouth with the back of his hand. "Dinner?"

Peter got the feeling Rich was a less-is-more kind of guy when it came to speaking. He glanced at his watch; it wasn't time for dinner. The day felt like it had been a century long, but it was only about noon.

"Dinner means lunch," Nat informed him. "We live in 1860 over here. We're going to go for a ride in the horseless carriage later, too."

Chuck shook his head, but his eyes twinkled. "Such a smart-ass."

Peter thought of Nel and grinned. "You need one in every group—comic relief."

"She's just like her mom."

Nat kept her smile on, but her fingers twisted in her lap. Chuck looked away and inspected the shelving unit. "Well, how about soup?"

"Just what I want on a hot summer afternoon," Nat said.

"I didn't say I was going to heat it up."

"Ugh."

Peter walked to the shelves and took stock. In amongst the packages and cans of food were some tomatoes, a sad-looking cucumber and zucchini. "You have a garden at the place you're fixing up?"

Chuck nodded. "Small one. Not enough to keep us going, but we've been going house to house. We'll have enough for the winter."

"Why not go to one of the Safe Zones?"

There was a grumble from the couch. "That's what I say," Rich said.

Chuck glanced at Nat and said, "It's not a good idea for now. Maybe in the spring."

Peter didn't ask any more. He held up a couple of packages of ramen noodles and grabbed the soy sauce and sesame oil that were in among the condiments. "I'm happy to make dinner, if you want."

"I'll take you up on that offer," Chuck said. "We're not the greatest chefs. Not that we have much to work with. You know how to cook?"

Peter nodded. Natalie helped light the stove, which sat by the open window. Grandma had never taken him camping, but he knew from the past months that using a camping stove indoors without adequate ventilation could kill them.

Ramen noodles were fast, and before long Peter had them cooled and tossed with the chopped vegetables, soy sauce and oil. It was too much to ask for some rice vinegar. Cassie's parents might have been a little over the top in their storage plans, but anything he'd needed had been in that basement. But, he reminded himself, they weren't really over the top; they'd kept him alive.

Peter set the bowl on the table. "Go ahead."

The three of them sat down and, judging by the silence and chewing, they liked it. He'd made cold ramen salad a few times this summer. His turn to cook had come up more and more frequently at the cabin, but he didn't mind. Watching everyone shovel in the food he'd made and fight good-naturedly over second helpings was more satisfying than eating it.

He'd always loved to cook. One of his earliest memories was standing on a kitchen chair in his parents' house in Westchester, his mom handing him a measuring cup loaded with flour to dump in the mixing bowl. As an adult, he'd eaten out more often than not, but he'd still cooked occasionally, mainly for girls he'd dated. Cassie had been no exception. Except that, unlike many others, she'd eat every morsel and sigh in delight.

Peter pulled one of the MREs out of his backpack, sat on the couch and placed it on the coffee table. The ramen salad was a much tastier option, but he wasn't going to eat their food. He was already taking up their space.

He imagined Bits and the others in the pickup, rolling along dirt roads. They might even be at Kingdom Come already, if they hadn't hit any trouble. But you didn't have to go looking for trouble anymore. All you had to do was get a flat tire or take a wrong turn, and you were dead. This was better than dead on a dumpster, for sure, but he would give anything to be in that truck. And not for his own safety; he wanted to be there in case anything else went wrong.

He wasn't very hungry anymore, but he opened the MRE to see what was inside. What to eat first—the big packet of slop, a smaller packet of something tasteless or jalapeno cheese spread with crackers? Decisions, decisions. The dessert didn't look bad. It was hard to mess up sugar.

"This is so totally yummy," Natalie called. She saw what he was doing and her eyebrows lowered. "Aren't you going to eat with us?"

Peter looked down at his food. "No, I'm fine."

"You can't cook and not eat," Chuck said. His gruff voice was friendly. "C'mon, Pete. You're making me look bad here."

He'd always hated being called Pete, but now he didn't mind. It meant someone liked you enough to give you a nickname, like how Cassie called him Petey sometimes. He walked to the table and pulled out the fourth chair, wondering why they had it. They might have brought it up to complete the set from the bathroom apartment. Maybe it was for Natalie's mother. He served himself a bit of ramen. Not as good as with the rice vinegar, but still tasty.

"We'll check out the street and get you going after dinner," Chuck said. "Where's that Safe Zone again?"

"Northeast Kingdom. Somewhere north of Lowell."

"I guess you need a vehicle. We have a few at the cabin all gassed up and working. We can take a ride there, see what we can spare. There are plenty of cars for the taking these days. Won't take us long to get another."

"I'd really appreciate that." Peter was almost giddy at the thought. He wouldn't be that far behind if he left this afternoon.

"Can I come?" Nat asked. Chuck shook his head. "Oh my God, Dad! Please? I'm dying of boredom. And it's so hot! I need a bath!"

She threw down her fork, crossed her arms and glared at her dad. He stared back, thick arms folded across his chest and eyes calm. He reminded Peter of John, the most implacable person he'd ever met. "What's the first rule?" Chuck asked.

"Safety," Nat said quietly, but her glare remained in place.

"And this is where you're safest."

"You said we were moving in by now, Daddy. It's safer there—after today you know it is! If you didn't come back, I'd be here with no fresh water and no truck. Then what would happen to me?"

Rich mumbled something that sounded like, "She has a point."

"You're right," Chuck said after a moment. "We could use some help at the cabin anyway. But you're working, not farting around."

Nat's eyes flicked to Peter. "Dad, you're so disgusting. We have company!"

CHAPTER 2

The road to the cabin was rutted like a washboard. It made Peter's neck, already a bit sore from a sleepless night and a whole lot of machete hacking, ache even more. After a few miles, when they hadn't passed anything but trees, he asked, "Was this your hunting camp or something?"

"Nope," Chuck said. "We brought it in piece by piece from other places. Rich and I built it ourselves."

The road ended at a clearing that bordered a large lake. The grass was overgrown, but over time Rich and Chuck's boots had trampled a path to where two rowboats and a canoe sat moored at the water's edge. There wasn't a cabin, though.

Natalie pressed her nose to the window and then smiled back over her shoulder. "It's on the island."

Peter followed her finger to the tree-shrouded island less than a quarter mile from the shore. There wasn't a visible sign of life, although he guessed that was the point. He helped load plastic bins full of food and toiletries into the boats and kept watch of the woods. It occurred to him that there were no extra vehicles, like Chuck had promised, and his fingers grazed the grip of the pistol in his holster. Rich and Chuck spoke in low voices while they worked. They seemed nice enough, but there was no reason to believe they planned to help him.

Chuck looked over at Peter as if he could read his thoughts and pointed across the lake with his chin. "There are a couple other roads on the north and east sides of the lake. We have trucks there in case this way's blocked."

Peter dropped his hand and tried not to look relieved. He was a pretty good judge of people. Not that that had stopped him from hanging out with superficial jerks most of his life, but at least he'd recognized what they were. And that he was one, too. It'd become painfully apparent after he met Cassie, who had no problem calling them on their asshole behavior.

The first time he'd met Cassie, at that bar in the city, he'd watched her for half the night. Her wavy, reddish-brown hair was loose, and she had a habit of tucking it behind one ear while she talked. She'd been there for a coworker's birthday celebration, along with Penny and Nelly. It was the type of bar he'd always frequented but she rarely had. Twelve dollar drinks made with twists of obscure fruit obviously were not her style, he remembered thinking, and her drink was the closest thing they had to a plain beer.

Most of the girls were dressed in designer clothes and heeled boots. Cassie wore a thirty dollar pair of jeans with beat-up black boots and a black tank top. She wasn't plain—the tank top showed off some nice cleavage and she wore makeup and earrings—she was just different. She touched people on their shoulders or arm while she spoke and listened to them with rapt attention. When she laughed, she threw her head back and let go. She didn't seem to care what the regular bar patrons thought of her, something of which Peter was envious.

He watched as several guys tracked her on her way to the bathroom; he wasn't the only one who was interested. In fact, she'd already shot one down with a shy smile and shake of her head.

When she went up to the bar for a round, he followed and leaned far enough away to not appear creepy. She glanced at him and then looked straight ahead until the bartender took her order. Peter quietly signaled the bartender to add them to his tab. After the drinks were lined up on the bar, she held out cash with her chipped blue fingernails until the bartender waved her off and pointed to Peter.

For a second she looked annoyed, but then she put on a smile and turned to him. "Thanks, that was very nice, but I really don't want you to pay for all these drinks."

"I insist," he said. She held out her money, but he crossed his arms and shook his head with a smile.

"Please, take the cash."

"Can't a guy buy a girl a drink?" he asked.

"Well, yeah, but a guy shouldn't buy a girl six drinks." She raised her eyebrows at his shrug. "You're not going to take my money, are you?"

"Nope."

"Well, then, thank you. That was very generous."

She shoved the money in her pocket and smiled, but he could tell she was uncomfortable. Maybe she thought he was trying to show off. Not that he was above that, but he hadn't been. It was harder to buy the one drink that was hers than to buy the whole round. He could have asked first, but then she had the option of refusing.

Peter moved close so she could hear him better. She smelled like roses and something fresh and green. "I'm Peter."

"Cassie. Hi." She smiled and tapped her fingers on the side of her beer bottle, as if at a loss of what to say next.

"Nice to meet you, Cassie."

Someone from her table must have motioned at her because she raised a finger, telling them to wait, and then looked at him again. "You, too."

She asked him about his work, and he saw her eyes glaze over when he went into his company's connections with lobbyists and congressmen. She was unfailingly polite and laughed when he said something humorous, but he could tell she was underwhelmed. Usually, it wouldn't have bothered him; most girls went for him, especially in a place like this, but there was an occasional no. That was to be expected. He didn't want to lose this one, though, and he could see he was.

She told him she'd grown up in Brooklyn, and he asked if her parents still lived there. Cassie froze for a second and then told him that they'd died two years before in a car accident. She tried to act like it was nothing, but he'd seen the pain in her eyes, the way she swallowed hard. He knew she was readying herself for that initial awkward moment and the apologies that inevitably followed.

"My family died in a car crash when I was twelve," he said. "My parents and my little sister." He almost didn't say what came into his head next, but he wanted her to know he understood. "It's like living in a house where the roof's been torn off, isn't it?"

She looked at him then—*really* looked at him—and nodded. Then she glanced toward the table where her friends sat staring. Her breath was warm when she spoke into his ear. "They're going to come after me if I don't give them their drinks. I'll be right back, okay?"

He nodded. She walked the drinks over to her friends and sat down next to Penny. For a moment he thought she wasn't coming back, but she'd left her beer on the bar. She whispered something in Penny's ear and then stood.

He'd felt so exposed after his parents died. Even with his grandma's pre-war apartment over his head. The world had suddenly become murderous and angry, a place where you had to grab what you could and run for cover. He couldn't believe he'd said that, especially to a stranger, but those words were why she was walking back to him now. All the free drinks and senators in the world wouldn't have impressed her. This girl was real, and he wanted real. But real was scary. Real was what could hurt you.

She pulled her barstool close and smiled, the same smile he'd seen her flash at her friends. The smile that lit up her face and made her hazel eyes with the dark lashes crinkle at the corners. It was the first time he'd mentioned the accident in years. Usually, if anyone cared enough to ask, he just said his parents were dead. And he never mentioned his sister, Jane. It not only made him want to cry, but it also triggered an irrational fear that someone would see his remorse and probe for details. But Cassie knew all too well what speaking about it took out of you—he'd seen it on her face.

They talked then, about things both serious and trivial. She told him about her job and how she loved introducing the neighborhood kids to art. How she'd stopped painting for herself. She asked him more questions about his work and then tilted her head, face flushed with her fourth beer. "Do you like it? It really doesn't sound like you do."

"No, I hate it," he said, a little more vehemently than he'd intended. It was true, but he'd never said it out loud.

Cassie jabbed him in the chest and her mouth dropped. "You *hate* it? Then why do you do it for a million hours a week? Life's too short for that crap. You should do what you love. Or *like*. Or can *tolerate*, at least."

He shrugged and wondered why, indeed. She laughed apologetically and waved a hand. "I should take my own advice. Don't listen to me."

A few hours into their conversation, a well-dressed, broad-shouldered guy with dirty blond hair walked up. He put a proprietary arm on Cassie's shoulder and looked Peter up and down, from his overpriced T-shirt to his expensive jeans and shoes, and didn't look impressed. "C'mon, you, we're leaving. It's almost last call."

"Nelly, this is Peter," Cassie said. "Peter, Nel."

"Thanks for the drink, man." Nel shook his hand and turned to Cassie. "Let's get a cab."

Cassie stood and touched Peter's hand. "It was nice talking to you. Let's both take my advice, okay?"

Peter didn't want her to go. He knew that with her overprotective friend looming in the background, she wouldn't give him her number. And if he gave her his business card he knew without a doubt she'd never call. "I'll put you in a car. We have one on call for the office. Stay for one more drink?"

She chewed her lip and looked at Nel. He gave her an *it's-your-life* shrug. Peter squeezed her hand and flashed his most affable smile. "I need more advice. Just think, I'll work forever at this job I hate and it'll be all your fault."

Her laugh rang out. "Okay. I can't be responsible for ruining your life."

"Text me when you're home," Nel said, and gave her a kiss on the cheek. The look he shot Peter before he left was one a big brother or father would have given. This was the guy to win over if he wanted Cassie to like him. He had a feeling that wasn't going to be easy.

They stayed until the bar closed. He thought about asking her to go to his place, but then she'd lump him in with every guy in every bar who'd ever tried to get her into bed. Not that he would've minded—from what he could see, those thirty dollar jeans would be a whole lot nicer on the floor—but he wasn't going to scare her off. They stood in the cool early morning air and talked while they waited for the car. Cassie lit a cigarette and explained she was down to one a day.

"But after a drink, or a whole host of drinks..." She blew the smoke into the air and sighed with pleasure.

Peter smiled, although he hated cigarettes. He didn't care what this girl did, as long as she did it near him. She was normal and weird and funny. And she was beautiful, in a way that grew on you instead of smacking you in the face. She was kind of like his mom, he realized, except for how he wanted to kiss her in a most unmotherly fashion, even with the cigarette she sucked down like it contained life-sustaining oxygen.

The car pulled up, and she stubbed out her cigarette before looking for a garbage can. "I can't throw it on the ground. It's a product of being raised by environmentalist parents."

He held out his hand. "I'll get it."

"Thanks." She deposited it in his palm and smiled nervously. "Okay, well, goodnight. It was really nice to meet you."

The black car's engine rumbled behind her. Peter had done this a million times, but he was genuinely afraid of being shot down for the first time since he was a teenager. He cleared his throat. "So, can I call you sometime? I might need more life coaching."

Cassie gripped the door handle. "I don't—I'm not really…" She looked up at the sky and shrugged. "You know what? Sure. I'll take my own advice."

She tapped her number into his phone and handed it back. Then, before he could even consider kissing her, she ducked into the backseat. "Goodnight, Petey."

He'd already tried to talk her out of calling him Petey, but apparently she was big on nicknames. "Goodnight, Cassandra."

She laughed because she'd mentioned earlier that no one ever called her by her full name. He watched the car drive away, grinning like an idiot; he already liked her more than he thought possible after only a few hours. He didn't even care that his hand smelled like an ashtray.

***

"We're all set," Chuck said, interrupting Peter's thoughts.

Peter shook off the memory. Even though things with Cassie had worked out differently than he had once hoped, it was still a good one. He never would've guessed that meeting her that night would save his life—in more ways than one. "Want me to take one of the rowboats?"

"If you don't mind rowing. We try not to run the engines unless we have to. We only use electric motors—quieter—but those still have to be charged."

"No problem."

Peter grabbed the oars and gained on the island quickly. Chuck and Nat were in the canoe, and Rich pulled the other rowboat with full, even strokes. Chuck pointed out a natural beach on the shore, and Peter rowed the boat up to the sandy area where he could disembark without soaking his boots.

"We usually pull the boats into the bushes," Chuck said, "but we'll unload and get you to a truck."

Peter followed them through the trees with his load and assessed the island. It was about an acre, maybe. He wasn't great at that kind of stuff, but he'd improved in recent months. These days, he could talk electrics with James, weapons with John and shoot the shit with Nel, all without feeling like he was in over his head or some sort of impostor.

A path led to a small cabin that was cobbled together out of mismatched boards and outfitted with solid storm windows that were perfect for a cold Vermont winter. The small deck at the front opened into a main room about twenty by twenty feet. There were two doors Peter assumed were bedrooms and another door by the kitchen. Maybe they had a bathroom. It was cozy and bright, even if the sheet-rock was unevenly taped and unpainted. Chuck caught him looking and knocked on the wall in the kitchen area. The kitchen was outfitted with an inset sink that had no faucet, shelves stocked with packaged food and a wood stove for heating and cooking.

"Not the prettiest house in the world, but, believe me, she's solid. And warm—insulation's inches thick. That's why we sheet-rocked. Nat's gonna paint it. Right, Nat?"

But Nat had already disappeared through a door into what was her room. Peter could see a mattress and dresser, along with posters on the wall and a shelf lined with books.

"How did you get all this here?" Peter asked.

"We have a larger boat hidden on the other side of the island. Uses a lot of gas, but for big jobs, it's the best."

Peter nodded and surveyed the rest of the house. You could tell it was designed by two guys, and as much as he abhorred the person he'd been, he couldn't help but want to redecorate it, just a little. The plain brown couch wasn't bad, but it should've been on the wall next to the windows, not stuck out in the middle, and the easy chairs should have been set near it to make a small living area. He'd arrange the dining table so that it opened the room. Paint those hideous brown wood side tables a light color. Some curtains to cover the black cloth they had for blackout shades. Some bright throw pillows. He didn't sit through Grandma's boring consultations with decorators and learn nothing.

"Nice place," Peter said.

"Yeah, well, it works," Chuck said, but Peter could tell he was proud. The same way Peter had been proud when he helped dig the ditch or fix the fence.

"Do you have solar?" he asked.

"Nah," Chuck said. "Don't know the first thing about it. We got ourselves a nice composting toilet and managed to get that working, but that's about it."

Peter nodded. He guessed they'd be fine, as long as they laid in enough wood and food. Living on an island was pretty clever, but it didn't leave a lot of space for growing things. He walked to the kitchen window and looked out at the garden. Some trees had been cleared to give it sun, but it would never produce enough to live on.

There were tomatoes, red and ripe, that made him think of Ana. She loved tomatoes. It now seemed ridiculous that he was thirty years old and hadn't kissed her, when it was so obvious she wanted him to. Ana was gorgeous, funny and, honestly, kind of insane. But he'd grown to appreciate that about her. There was hardly any gray; her world was all black and white. This was great when she was on your side, not so much if she wasn't. But even when she drove him crazy, he still admired her single-mindedness.

Peter had spent almost two decades afraid that no one would like the real him—Grandma certainly hadn't. He loved how Ana didn't care; either you liked her or you didn't, and she didn't waste time trying to convince you either way. And now that she'd matured out of her bratty little sister phase, everyone did like her. She was strong, opinionated and a fervent zealot of zombie killing, but she'd softened, too. It was obvious how much she loved them all, even when she tried to hide it behind her flippant grin and ever-present cleaver.

He hadn't wanted to start something with Ana because he could only imagine how awkward it'd be to have to live with *two* ex-girlfriends. Finally, last night, Cassie had ordered him to be happy and to stop wasting time. And he'd been about to do just that, until the Lexers showed.

Maybe, when he next saw Ana, he'd take her face in his hands and kiss her, finally run his fingers down that silky brown skin. He wished he'd at least gotten that slow dance he'd asked Ana for last night, the one intended to break the tension that had sprung up between them in recent weeks. He sighed; he could wish all he wanted, but the only way to make any of it come true was to get himself to Kingdom Come.

"You have any potatoes in?" Peter asked to fill in the silence that had grown as he'd gazed out the window. He was chock-full of introspection today, but he guessed a near-death experience could do that to you.

"No, we started late. Spent the first part of summer just surviving, you know?"

"Yeah. You should try to find some in the supermarkets or houses. I don't know much about gardening, but you can at least try to save them for seed potatoes next spring. You can plant potatoes in a small area, and then let them grow vertically. Just add some more soil or hay on top."

"That's a good idea. We don't have much space. Next year we'll start a garden on the mainland, if we're still here."

Another couple of trips finished the unloading. Chuck thanked him and said, "Let's get you on your way."

"I'm coming," Nat announced and walked out of hiding. She'd changed into a bathing suit with a sundress over top. "I want to go for a swim with a bar of soap."

"All right," Chuck said. "I have some supplies for the trucks, so I'll take the rowboat. Pete, you want to go in the canoe with Natalie, so she doesn't paddle in circles?"

Natalie stuck out her tongue at her dad and giggled. Now that she was there, she seemed relaxed; they all did. He could hear Rich out in the yard, humming under his breath and talking to a dog Peter had glimpsed when they'd approached the cabin.

The trees lessened the heat; maybe the water did too. What was a beastly hot day in Bennington was warm and breezy on the island. Peter shoved his button-down in his bag as they left for the boats. He'd wear his jacket on the road, for protection, but there was no reason to get all sweaty in the boat.

Rich rounded the corner of the house. "You leaving?"

"Yeah," Peter said, and held out his hand. "Thanks for all your help. You don't know how grateful I am."

Rich shook his hand with a nod and disappeared to the back.

"Uncle Rich is a man of few words," Natalie said. She picked her way down the trail in her flip-flops. "Can you not see why I'm starting to go crazy? Can't you stay for a few days?"

"Peter wants to get to his little girl," Chuck said. He pulled a life vest off a tree branch by the boats and held it out to Nat. "Put this on."

"I didn't wear one on the way out, Dad. I've been able to swim since I was, like, five."

"That's because it was out here. If it'd been on shore, you would've worn it. What's the first rule?"

Nat didn't answer, so Peter did. "Safety. It's a good one."

"Traitor!" Natalie said, but she laughed and clicked the vest on.

The trucks were a bit farther away than where they'd arrived. Peter dug his paddle into the water as they got close. Nat was paddling, but he hardly needed her. He'd be behind the wheel of a truck in less than fifteen minutes and would drive all night until he reached Kingdom Come.

Natalie hopped out of the canoe before they reached the shore and then splashed in knee-deep water. This was another grassy clearing, with a similar dilapidated road that led into the woods. Parked on the grass were a pickup and a Mercedes G-Class.

"Nice truck," Peter said to Chuck, who'd pulled alongside him in the rowboat. "That yours from before?"

Chuck laughed. "Oh, sure, a hundred grand was a drop in the bucket. Parked it next to my Rolls. You know cars?"

"Not much. But I had an S600."

"Nice," Chuck said with a low whistle. "You must've been doing okay."

"I guess," Peter said. Except he hadn't been. He didn't like this new world, but he was possibly the only person who felt that they were better off than before.

"It was at a big house outside Manchester. Only way I'd ever own a—"

A shrill scream echoed. Nat had slipped out of the water and behind the trucks, where her father had warned her not to go without his 'all clear.' Her palms hit the truck's hood, and Peter caught a glimpse of her terrified face before she slid off. Chuck was quick, but Peter was quicker. He leapt across the grass, machete drawn.

The Lexer had Nat by her vest. It pulled her steadily backward despite her bare feet that scrabbled on the ground. Peter knew he had one chance to get the Lexer off; its teeth were perilously close to her neck, and there was more movement in the woods.

"Get down! Duck!" he ordered Nat, who reacted immediately.

He swung the machete into its mouth, bisecting the head, the top of which flew into the trees. The next few headed for where Natalie lay under the corpse of the first Lexer, its hands still tangled in her straps. He drove the machete into an eye, flipped the blade to his left hand and spun to shoot the two behind him at point blank range. It was better to avoid using a gun and calling everything within a few miles your way, but sometimes it was unavoidable. Thank God for Ana and her insanity. All that practice was paying off.

Chuck had taken out the last two with his pistol, and now he was bent over Nat, disentangling her from beneath the Lexer. He didn't see the one who came out from behind the other truck. Peter fired a perfect kill shot, but the bullet didn't stop the Lexer's forward momentum enough to keep it from knocking Chuck off balance and into Peter's ankle.

Searing pain shot up his leg when Chuck's bulk hit, even with his boot for support. Peter put an arm on the truck and waited for the initial pain to pass while Chuck lifted Nat to her feet. The back of her head was wet with brains, and her pixie face was bright pink from the struggle to catch her breath. Chuck undid the life vest and inspected every inch of her, then raised disbelieving eyes to where Peter stood.

"Jesus Christ," he said. His face was almost as flushed as Nat's. "They had her. Jesus."

Chuck opened the truck door and threw Natalie in. He slammed it and turned to face the woods, then fell against the truck. "I wouldn't have made it in time."

"You would've," Peter said.

Whether or not that was true, Peter wasn't sure, but Chuck needed to believe it. Chuck stared straight ahead. He wasn't shaking, but he looked like a man reliving a nightmare. Peter knew; he'd been there.

"I don't know," Chuck said. He looked Peter in the eye, not ashamed of the tears that filled his. "Thank you for saving my baby. You want that G-Class, it's all yours."

Peter gave a small laugh but winced when he put weight on his foot. Now that the adrenaline was wearing off, the initial pain was getting a whole lot worse. His boot felt much too tight.

"I nailed you in that ankle, didn't I?" Chuck asked. "Let's take a look."

Peter sat on a rock to unlace his boot and remove his sock. His ankle was already swollen and an angry pink.

"God, I'm sorry," Chuck said.

Peter shook his head. It was his right foot, too. He'd drive with his left if he had to. "It's all right. It'll go down soon."

Chuck rubbed his beard and grimaced. "I don't know. That looks bad. Did you feel or hear a crack?"

"No, it just bent the wrong way."

"I guess that's good. Rich could tell us more—he's a nurse."

So, non-speaking, classical music-playing, flannel shirt-wearing Rich was a nurse. Peter smiled despite the pain and the sinking feeling that his ankle was about to throw an extra-large wrench into his plans. "Must have a hell of a bedside manner. Strong but silent?"

"You'd be surprised." Chuck guffawed and turned a fatherly look on him. "I think you should come back, at least for the night. It'd be better to leave in the morning anyway."

Peter's chest tightened. He should have been saying goodbye and heading down the road right now. But, he reminded himself, he should have been dead on a dumpster right now, so another night was a lot better than what could have been. He pushed himself off the rock and gingerly placed the toes of his right foot on the ground. "Yeah. I guess so."

CHAPTER 3

Peter lay with his foot propped on the arm of the couch while Rich looked it over. Although his hands were gentle, it was enough to make Peter grit his teeth. It hurt almost as much as breaking his arm when he was nine.

"No crunching feeling when I move it?" Rich asked.

"No."

"Well, I can't say for certain, but I think it's a fairly bad sprain. You should stay off it for a week, then minimal movement for another week or more, depending. I'll get some cold water from the lake for you to soak in and then we'll wrap it up."

"I wanted to leave in the morning."

Rich had been businesslike during his examination, but now he squatted near Peter's propped-up head with a sigh and a gentle voice. "I know you do. But you won't be doing yourself any favors. What if you have to get out of the truck? The roads north aren't all clear, even the small ones. I know, I've tried them. You can't run with that ankle."

Peter watched the treetops through the window and bit his cheek hard. It was a good defensive maneuver for when you didn't want to cry. And the first and last time he'd cried in years had been on the front porch of Cassie's cabin.

"If you do too much too soon on that ankle it could worsen and never heal right," Rich continued. He gestured out the window. "This is not a situation where a man wants a permanently weak ankle or a limp, you know?"

"Okay," Peter said. He knew Rich was right. "I'm sorry I'm stuck here. I know you don't have supplies to spare."

"We can always get more," Rich said. He blinked a few times. "What we can't get is another Natalie. I'll go for that water."

He clapped Peter's shoulder and went humming out the door. It sounded like Beethoven's 7th.

***

The next day was hot, which only intensified the heat in his ankle. Natalie walked out of her room and perched on the end of the couch. Her eyes were puffy, and she looked exhausted despite having slept through from yesterday evening.

"I know I said thank you," she said. "But thank you again, for saving me…" She looked down at her lap. "Sorry I screwed up your plans to leave. My dad would ground me, except I'm already stuck here."

She gave him a sheepish look from under her hair, and Peter laughed. "I'm glad I was there. That's how fast it happens. That's why your dad has that first rule, you know."

Nat sighed. "I know."

"Anyway, we're even. You saved me and I saved you back. All right?"

"I didn't think of that," Nat said with a grin. "But, I'm still your servant until you leave. Dad's orders. Can I get you anything?"

Peter didn't want to make a sixteen year-old girl help him to the bathroom. It would be embarrassing for both of them. "I just need to do morning stuff, you know. Brush my teeth…"

She moved to one of the side tables and came back with a stick that spread into a V at the top. "Cane for you. Dad said he was making one."

"Thanks."

Peter hobbled to the toilet. It stood alone in a tiny room the size of a closet. It didn't smell; supposedly everything went into a tank outside somewhere and became compost. They'd had a flush toilet at Cassie's, but he'd bet flush toilets were going to be a distant memory soon.

He dug around in his daypack. There was a toothbrush and toothpaste in a plastic bag at the bottom. He was pretty sure Cassie was responsible for that, considering that there was floss, too. Their daypacks held essential items, in case you had to leave your big pack behind. He had a couple of MREs, a flashlight, an emergency blanket and poncho, water, ammo, an extra knife and shirt, and some medical supplies. Only Cassie would think a toothbrush met the same qualifications as those things. He loaded up the toothbrush. By the time he spit and rinsed he felt cleaner all over. It was an illusion, of course, but maybe she was onto something.

His ankle was on fire, so he made his way to the couch and sat with his foot outstretched on the coffee table. He wasn't used to sitting, especially now. There was always something to do.

Chuck came in with a plate and steaming mug. "Coffee and peanut butter crackers. Odd mix, I know, but we use things as they expire."

"Thanks." He sipped the coffee. It was black, which was fine, and the crackers were pretty good.

Chuck sat on the couch. "Did you see Natalie?"

"Yeah. Was she under orders to apologize? If so, she did." Peter finished chewing and swallowed the crackers with a swig of coffee. "Don't go too hard on her."

"She didn't listen," Chuck said, his face hard. "I almost lost her."

"I think she learned her lesson. Has she ever had close contact with Lexers?"

"That's a funny name for them. Lexers?"

"That's what the Army was calling them. For the LX in Bornavirus LX."

"I guess we just call them zombies," Chuck said. "That's what they are. I don't see the sense in another name."

"Maybe it's kind of like calling lollipops something different, like suckers."

"Change it up a little?" Chuck asked with a smile. "So you don't get bored?"

Peter laughed. "Exactly."

"No, she never did. She's shot at them from a distance, when all this started, but not since then. Maybe she should have, but I don't think it's worth the risk. She knows how to use a gun, has since she was little. I'll make sure she has one at all times from here on out."

Peter finished the crackers and coffee. That was breakfast, and once Chuck left to do his work, Peter was going to be bored. "Is there anything you need done that I can do from here?"

Chuck thought a moment and said he'd be back. Rich came in with the dog, who looked a bit like John's dog, Laddie. Suddenly, those crackers weren't sitting so well. It was Peter's fault Laddie had been killed; he still felt horrible about that. No one held it against him anymore, but he'd never totally forgive himself.

The dog rushed over, tail wagging like crazy. The second Peter made eye contact, it jumped on the couch and set its head in his lap.

"Go 'head and make yourself comfortable, Jack," Rich said to the dog. "You want me to get him off?"

Peter gave Jack a good scratch behind the ear. He'd never had a dog, but he'd always wanted one. "That's okay, I like him."

"All right. I want to take a look at your ankle."

Rich took Peter's foot in his lap and unwrapped the bandage while Nat hovered over him. When the bandage was off, she scrunched up her nose. "It looks like a zombie foot!"

It did. It was swollen and purple-gray, just like a Lexer. "Looking better than it did, in terms of swelling," Rich said. "That's good. Keep it up. Nat will get you anything you need."

"I already told him I'm his indentured servant," she said, and turned to Peter. "How about a board game?"

"I think your dad's getting me something to work on."

Natalie bowed. "Yes, master."

Rich looked up from his bandaging. "I can't believe your daddy never spanked you. Maybe I should." He swatted a hand and she ran away laughing. It looked like it was an old joke from the way they both smiled.

"All right," Rich said. "I'll be outside. Make sure to take some more ibuprofen."

After two more days, Peter was sure he'd sharpened every knife within a fifteen-mile radius. His ankle was a little better, in that he could stand for longer periods of time, but he still couldn't walk at anything resembling a normal pace. Rich told him to be patient, but it was impossible. Everyone was waiting for him at Kingdom Come, except they didn't know they were waiting; they were likely mourning.

Chuck had given him some other odd jobs, but there was only so much he could do from the couch—the same one he'd had Natalie help move under the windows. They'd moved the chairs too, so at night everyone could sit and talk or play a game.

Natalie had just won Monopoly for the third night in a row when Chuck said, "Rich and I are thinking of going out tomorrow. We'd be gone for a night. Going for food. And I'm going to check on those potatoes, like you said, Peter."

"Will you get paint, Daddy?" Nat asked. "I'll start on painting. And get some fabric for curtains and furniture paint, too. Like white or something. Oh, and a sewing machine."

She gave Peter a thumbs up; the last two days had been full of decorating discussions. She might have been his servant, but he was her captive audience, and he had a feeling she was quite happy with the arrangement.

"I'll see what we can do. You sure you're okay here, Nat?"

"Of course. Peter'll keep me company."

Chuck shot Peter an amused look that might have been tinged with sympathy. "All right. Let's get to bed, it's late."

Peter brushed his teeth and lay on the couch wearing a pair of Chuck's pajama pants. When Natalie's door closed, Chuck sat on the edge of the coffee table with his hands clasped. "Listen, Pete, I have a favor to ask." He waited for Peter's nod and continued. "If we don't come back, would you take Nat with you when you leave?"

"You'll come back, Chuck."

"You never know. Just in case. I want to know she'll have someone looking out for her. I trust you would."

"Of course I would," Peter said. He felt a rush of warmth that this man trusted him with his daughter. No one had ever even asked him to housesit. Of course, his wealthy friends would never have needed him to, but still. "You have my word."

Chuck nodded once. "All right, then. Thank you." He walked into the bedroom he shared with Rich and closed the door softly.

***

The next day it was just Nat, Peter and Jack. By noon they'd already gone swimming with a bar of soap, as Nat called it. The cold water felt great on his ankle, and the soap was great everywhere else. Natalie wrapped his foot up the way Rich had taught her, and they sat in the living room reading. Nat had a million books in her room, but Peter was reading one of the guys' mysteries.

Natalie held a dog-eared copy of *Twilight* and read it as if it were the first time, although she'd told him she almost knew them by heart.

"So, what's the big deal with those *Twilight* books?"

Natalie lowered it and sighed. "It's all just so romantic. And who wouldn't want to live forever and be as super strong as a vampire?"

"Well, it'd be better than being a zombie."

"It's the closest I'm getting to romance anyway," Nat said. She flopped back in her chair. "I'd even take a normal guy at this point."

"Wow, a normal guy? That's really desperate."

"Shut up!" Nat giggled. Then she leaned forward. "So, you were with some girls when I saw you. That one, the one next to you who held your hand, is that your girlfriend?"

"That's my ex-girlfriend, Cassie," Peter said.

"Why'd you break up? Details!"

There was no way she was getting details. "It just didn't work out."

Natalie blew her hair off her forehead and rolled her eyes. "Thanks, that was such a great story. Well, how about the other girls?"

Peter raised an eyebrow. "I'm not discussing this with you. You do know you're sixteen and I'm thirty, right?"

"Please," Nat begged. "No TV, no movies, I need some entertainment in my life."

Peter shook his head. She slumped in her chair but perked back up a moment later. "Okay, then, I'll guess. That one with the short hair—what's her name?"

"Ana," Peter answered because he couldn't think of a good reason not to. Ana had frozen in shock when she'd realized that they were leaving him behind. He'd opened his mouth to tell her that it would be all right—he'd be all right, as long as she and the others were safe—but there hadn't been time.

Natalie watched him for a moment before a grin spread across her face. "You like Ana—I can tell!"

Peter shrugged noncommittally, but she clapped her hands and screeched. "So, what'd Cassie think of that?"

Peter decided to answer; he had a feeling she'd be hounding him all night if he didn't. "She thought it was a good idea."

"What?" Nat screamed in disbelief. "Really?"

Peter couldn't help it; he laughed until tears rolled. Natalie grinned and jumped up to sit next to him. "So everyone was friends?"

"Yeah, everyone was friends," Peter said. "Cassie's probably my best friend." Cassie knew more about him than anyone else in the world, even Ana.

"Were you guys in love, ever?"

"I was in love with her," Peter said, and he felt a twinge of that old hurt, "but she wasn't in love with me."

"Just like Jacob," Nat said sadly.

"Like who?"

"*Twilight*. The werewolf. Does Cassie love someone else, like how Bella loves Edward? That's the vampire."

"Yeah, she does," Peter said. The mood was growing somber, and he didn't want it to. He was fine. It had all worked out the way it was supposed to. "But he's not a vampire. I hear he's pretty nice."

"So do you still love her?"

"I do, but in a different way. I want her to be happy. It's complicated."

Natalie's eyes brimmed with tears. Peter patted her shoulder. "Listen, goofball, it's not sad. When I make it there, you know who I want to be with?" Natalie shook her head. "Ana."

"But do you love her?"

"I think so." He studied the wall and wished Rich and Chuck were around to put an end to this conversation.

"But do you still love Cassie, too?"

Peter sighed. She wouldn't stop harping on this, and he didn't know how to explain it to this girl who thought everything was a love triangle in a young adult novel. He didn't expect or even want to be with Cassie, but he still loved her in that way that love can turn into deep affection. "Yeah. Sort of."

Nat bounced on the couch cushions, eyes suddenly dry. "Bella loves Jacob, too, but it's different. Maybe like how you mean. You really need to read *Twilight*."

Peter couldn't think of any situation where *Twilight* would be required reading. "I think I'm doing all right without Bella's help. But thanks."

He picked up his book to signal that the conversation about his love life was over. Natalie ripped the mystery out of his hands and tossed it across the room. Then she put *Twilight* on his lap and moved his cane out of reach. "Please? Just read the first few chapters and I promise I'll give you your other book back if you want. I have no one to talk to about this stuff! Please, please read it!"

"You are a pain in the butt," Peter said. It was supposed to be a stern voice, but it was obvious from her wide smile that she wasn't buying it. He would read the damn book, if only because that hopeful face she made reminded him of Bits. "Fine, I'll read it."

She squealed and did a victory dance. He was being played like a violin.

CHAPTER 4

Chuck and Rich still weren't back by the time he was almost through with *New Moon* and the sun was going down on day two. Natalie stood by the window, her hand resting on Jack's head.

"I'm sure they're okay," Peter said, although he wasn't. "They know I'm here and you're safe. So they might have stayed an extra night if they needed to."

Nat nodded and continued her vigil. When the sun had left the sky, she said she was going to bed. Peter read a chapter of *Eclipse*, then blew out the lamp and sat in the dark, listening for the sound of oars in the water that never came.

Natalie woke him the next morning with coffee. "I think you're right. I gave them a whole list of stuff to get, so they're probably doing that." Her mouth was tight, though, and the coffee mug shook.

"Hey, don't cry, sweetie." Peter sat up and patted the couch beside him. "I have a feeling they're fine. I really do."

She dropped beside him and folded under his arm like a baby bird. She may have been sarcastic, sixteen and yearning for paranormal romance, but right now, sobbing into his shoulder, she was a scared little girl. Bits had lots of people to protect her, and he was glad he was there to give Chuck the same peace of mind.

They sat like that until Peter's coffee was cold and Nat had cried herself out. When he finally rose, his ankle felt a bit better than the day before. He couldn't run, or even walk fast, but it was healing. Another week or two and he'd be on his way. Maybe with Natalie in tow, but he hoped not. She needed her dad.

Afternoon brought a rainstorm, one that the men would probably wait out instead of rowing across the lake in. Peter and Nat were deep into a game of Scrabble when footsteps sounded on the deck and Chuck came in dripping.

"Daddy!" Nat yelled and threw herself into her father's arms. As he imagined Bits doing the same, Peter bit his cheek.

"Sorry about that," Chuck said to Peter. "God, I wish we could've called. We got stuck in a store, had to wait them out. But everything's fine." He took Nat's face in his hands and looked down at her, eyes shining. "Everything's fine. Okay?"

Her head moved up and down, and when he asked for help moving the stuff to the cabin, she threw on a coat and ran down to the water.

"Be careful out there," Chuck said before he followed. "We were surrounded by hundreds of 'em. We'll make a couple more trips while you're here, if that's all right, and then we're sticking close until the winter. Maybe they'll freeze."

"I hope so. Do what you have to do. I'm not going anywhere yet." And Peter certainly wasn't leaving Nat alone until he knew they were there to stay.

***

Peter sat in a chair and rolled the paint roller across the wall. He had the bottom half, Natalie the top. The cabin was much brighter now. Rich had chosen a premixed light blue, and it was turning out to be the perfect shade. He'd also gotten some white curtains and curtain rods, which he'd hung up. Once Peter finished the second coat on his half of the walls, he moved his chair to the sewing machine they'd set up on the table.

"So, how does that work with no electricity?" Natalie asked.

"You know my long leather gloves?" She nodded. "Well, Cassie made those for everyone using a sewing machine. You just turn the knob on the side and it sews for you. That's all the electricity does."

"Cool."

Peter picked up the blue and brown modern floral fabric Rich had picked out. It looked like something from a magazine and matched the paint and the couch and chairs suspiciously well. "So, tell me about your uncle. He hardly ever speaks, dresses like a redneck, but he listens to classical music and managed to pick out the perfect fabric."

He wasn't worried that Rich would hear, since they'd left this morning on another run. Tomorrow would be Peter's sixteenth day there, and he was babying his ankle so he would be able to leave sooner rather than later. Rich said he was probably looking at another week there, as long as he didn't overtax it.

"Uncle Rich was always like that. My grandma listened to classical music and was always redecorating. I guess he ended up liking it. My mom probably would've liked it if my dad was a little more like him."

Peter thought about asking where her mom was, but the way her eyes grew unfocused and she bit her lip decided him against it.

"He wasn't always quiet, though," Nat continued. "He went back to his house to get my cousins and aunt and came back quiet. That's what my dad says: He came back quiet. He won't tell us anything, except that it was too late."

"Oh."

Peter imagined the mess Rich might have found and tried to put it out of his mind. That could certainly make a person quiet. He measured and cut the fabric to cover the extra bed pillows they'd cut into squares and read the instructions for the machine. He'd never sewn before, but it seemed easy enough.

Nat wiped a splotch of paint off her cheek. "You think Uncle Rich is weird, but you're like him, you know. You killed all those zombies like a superhero, but here you are, decorating the house with me. And I know your clothes were super expensive before."

"You know, you're right," Peter said with a laugh. He hadn't realized that he might be considered a walking contradiction these days.

An hour later he sighed and laid the first uneven pillowcase on the floor. He was going to have to thank Cassie for the gloves again. How she'd fit together the strips of leather with such perfect seams, figured out the elastic and connected them to the gloves they'd found was amazing. He could barely sew a square, he'd just learned. The bobbin was still a complex mystery, although he'd gotten it to work. Natalie sat next to him, and together they made the second pillowcase a little more square than the first. The third was decent, and the fourth was almost perfect. They placed them on the couch and chairs and admired their handiwork.

"It never would've looked this nice without your help," Natalie said. "We just have to spray paint the tables and we're done."

"Tomorrow. Let's get some sleep."

Natalie stood on her tiptoes and hugged him goodnight, like he was family. He stole her nose and pretended to put it in his back pocket. She humored him with a smile, the same way Bits did when he stole her nose. Even at half of Nat's age, Bits was too old for Got Your Nose.

Nat raised her eyebrows. "Am I supposed to ask for it back or something?"

"Nope." Peter tapped his pocket. "I have quite the collection. I'm not giving it up."

"Wow, and here I thought you were cool. You're just as dorky as my dad."

Peter smiled. "I'll take that as a compliment."

"Goodnight, weirdo." Nat giggled and headed for her room but turned at the door. "My dad told me if they don't come back that I would go with you to Kingdom Come. He wanted me to know, just in case."

"That's right," Peter said. "But, don't worry, they'll be back."

"I know. I just didn't want you to worry about telling me." She put her hands on her hips. "Now, would you finish *Breaking Dawn*, already? I'm dying over here! We need to discuss!"

Nat skipped into her room and shut the door behind her. She'd gone from something as terrible as admitting her dad may never come back to demanding a *Twilight* symposium. Teenage girls were so strange, and he was extremely glad he was no longer a teenage boy. How any of them could compete with a sparkly vampire was beyond him. One day Bits would be a teenage girl, he realized, and picked up the book with a grimace. He should know what he was getting into.

***

Peter had circled the island over and over for days, until his ankle wasn't sore. He'd run around in the brush as much as was possible. It was time, and when he announced his intention to leave the next day everyone looked disappointed. He would have stayed if he'd had nowhere to go, since he'd grown fond of them these past weeks. But September was almost half over, and he wanted to reach Kingdom Come before the snow started.

"I knew it was coming," Chuck said, out on the deck after supper. "And thanks for staying longer than you needed to, so Nat wouldn't be alone. We'll miss you, Pete."

"You could all come. I know you've put a lot of work into this place, but apparently this Safe Zone really is safe."

Chuck sighed. "Next year, maybe, if we still need Safe Zones. We can't go just yet."

"Can I ask why?"

"Natalie's mom. I'm waiting for her." Chuck's face softened, and he smiled when Peter failed at hiding the thought that she wasn't coming from showing on his face. "I know, it sounds crazy. But I want to give her more time."

"Where was she?"

"I'm not sure. We were separated, and it was Nat's weekend with me. By the time I got to her house there was no sign of her. She's a smart lady. She could still be okay. Not like Rich's..."

Peter nodded. "Nat told me."

"She doesn't know the details. From what Rich said, it looked like his wife attacked his kids. My nephew was dead, but my niece and sister-in-law were still there. He had to—"

Peter filled in the silence. "Shit."

"Yeah. Anyway, I've left notes everywhere my wife might go, telling her we're here. This is where we used to make out in high school." Chuck laughed. "So I could leave notes without being specific."

"I hope she comes."

Chuck kicked a rock off the steps. "Me too. I know she will, if she can. Maybe not for me, but for Natalie she'd do anything."

"Well, you know where I'll be if you change your mind."

"I bet you can't wait," Chuck said. The straight line of his mouth curved a tiny bit. "Your little girl is there, and I've heard a bit about the others from Nat."

"I can only imagine what she told you."

Chuck clapped his back and howled. "She said she doesn't know how any girl wouldn't love you back. I think you may have beat out Edward."

Peter laughed but said quietly, "Well, I was a jerk. That's why any girl wouldn't have loved me back."

"Yeah," Chuck said with a sigh. "I could've done a lot of things differently. I still love my wife, and I'm hoping I get a chance to make it right. You've got that chance, to make things different. Take it."

Peter looked at Chuck's broad, kind face. He was the kind of person Peter might have disregarded as simple a few months ago, if he'd even deigned to notice him. He hadn't been overtly rude, but he'd treated people like they were invisible much of the time.

Maybe because he'd felt invisible. That's what he'd said to Cassie one night. She'd told him it wasn't true, but he'd pretended to fall asleep so as not to cry. The next morning Cassie tried to bring it up again, and he'd seen the impatience and hurt in her eyes when he shot her down. He'd known then that it was his last chance, and he hadn't taken it.

That's what he'd done the whole time they dated. Whenever he felt her pull away, he'd open up just enough for her to see the guy from the night they met. Then he'd get scared and distance himself again. It must have driven her crazy.

Well, he wasn't scared anymore. There was a hell of a lot of other stuff to be scared of these days. Machetes and guns were useful, but the only thing that could really allay the fear was people. And for the first time in eighteen years, he had people. He had a daughter, a best friend, a possible girlfriend and the rest of his new family. He was lucky to have gotten one more chance to make things different and not fucked it up for the thousandth time.

Peter clapped Chuck's shoulder in return. "I already have."

***

The next morning, Rich, Chuck and Nat stood beside the truck and watched Peter throw his bag into the passenger seat well. "You sure you don't want the Mercedes?" Chuck asked. "You can have it."

"I'm sure," Peter answered. He grinned and kicked a tire. "Maybe I'm more of a pickup guy now."

Natalie threw herself at him. "I'll miss you!"

"Don't wait around for any sparkly vampires," he whispered in her ear.

"I'd be on Team Peter, if you weren't so ancient," Nat said and pulled away, eyes sparkling.

"Thanks," he said. "I think."

He wished they were coming. On their way up to Cassie's cabin, they'd left the Washingtons at the campground with promises to meet up, but they never showed. The chances of seeing Chuck, Rich and Nat again were slim to none. He understood Chuck's reasoning, his desperate hope, but people needed to band together. It might be the only way to win back the world from the Lexers.

He held out his hand. "Thanks for all the nursing, Rich."

"Thanks for helping around the cabin," Rich said with one of his rare smiles. "It looks real nice. My brother would've dragged me over the coals if I'd suggested any of it."

Chuck punched Rich's shoulder and gave Peter a back-thumping hug. "You be safe out there."

Peter nodded and got into the pickup. He spread the map, marked with roads Rich knew to be clear, out on the seat beside him. It would get him a third of the way there. After that, he was on his own. He put the truck in drive.

"So long, lollipop!" Nat called.

She'd remembered. He laughed and waved one last time. "So long, lollipops."

And then he started down the road.

CHAPTER 5

A t first the roads took him past widely-spaced houses and fields
choked with weeds. It all looked so desolate. Even the houses
that didn't have signs of struggle—broken windows or bodies out
front—looked lonely. He felt like the last human on Earth. He
wasn't, of course, which was the only thing that kept him sane. He
tried to imagine someone driving blindly along these roads, hoping
to find something besides the small groups of Lexers he'd passed,
and saw how it would be possible to give up. The old Peter probably
would have, but not him.

He knew there was good out there in the world, hidden in places
like campgrounds and tiny lake islands. And even if he arrived at
Kingdom Come to find they hadn't made it there, he wouldn't give
up. The thought made the inside of his cheek bloody, but he had to
entertain it. It was reality.

Okay, that had been enough entertaining of reality. He
concentrated on the road. It'd turned into one and a half lanes of
rutted, dried mud. If Rich hadn't assured him that it went through, he
would have turned back by now. Finally, he came out onto a road
that looked like it had been driven on by something other than
logging trucks. He followed it north, branching onto smaller roads
with the occasional tiny town center and groups of Lexers loitering
around the general stores and empty intersections.

He'd just passed the point of charted territory when he hit his
first road blockage. How a traffic jam came to be in the middle of
this stretch of dirt road was beyond him, but there were four cars and
no way around. He looked into the woods to make sure they were

empty and kept the scuffing of his boots to a minimum while he meandered around the scene. There was a one-armed body in a car, head leaning against the window.

He pushed between it and the car alongside and almost lost his shit when the body moved. Its head slammed against the window, the leathery skin of its mummified face leaving flakes in its wake. It knelt on the seat, its red-veined eyes hungry. Peter breathed out and watched it struggle. Sometimes it felt as though this were a dream— a nightmare, really. That there was such a thing as zombies was unbelievable. Maybe Nat *should* hold out for that sparkly vampire.

He walked to the lead car, a silver Prius angled across the road. The cars behind had slammed into it when it'd stopped short after hitting something. That something was under its front wheel, still alive. Or undead, take your pick. It reached its arms up and clacked its teeth, so eager that it almost separated from its legs pinned under the tire. Peter stabbed his machete through its eye.

The Prius's door was open, but the keys were gone. There was no other way to shift it into neutral that he knew of. He bet John could've done it. The most Peter knew about cars was how to change a tire, check the oil and things like that—he wasn't a complete moron—but put him under a hood and he was lost. Feeling like an idiot for trying, he attempted to push the Prius out of the way. He might have been a superhero, according to Nat, but there was no way the car was moving.

He passed the car with the zombie inside and gave it the finger when it went crazy again. Juvenile, maybe, but it made him feel better. It was time to backtrack. Four hours into the drive and he was only a third of the way. He'd known it wasn't going to be a piece of cake, but this was more than a little discouraging. If all the roads were in similar shape, he was going to have to find a bike. Actually, that wasn't a bad idea. He'd backtrack, look for a bike and throw it in the truck, just in case.

There was a bike in the garage of a house somewhere south of Rutland. It was tall enough for his six feet, and the tires weren't flat. It even had panniers and a small pump. He thought of going into the house, but after knocking and being answered by a series of thumps, he decided to play it safe. He had enough food for a few days. There was no sense in asking for trouble. Ana probably would've argued for going in, just for laughs. He shook his head and smiled.

Banana—that was Penny and Cassie's nickname for Ana, and it was an apt one.

Lexers had passed while he was in the garage, and he checked carefully before he loaded the bike and drove away. Judging by how many he'd seen in this fairly isolated area, heading to a town the size of Rutland would be a very bad idea.

He headed east and north along dirt roads and roads that might as well have been dirt, with all the patched asphalt, but at least they were passable. As long as the road twisted through farmland, there was a shoulder or grass on which to skirt the inevitable abandoned cars. It was when the road narrowed in the woods that it became an issue. Google Earth would've come in handy, since the map didn't show the terrain a road traveled through. Good thing there weren't a lot of trees in Vermont. He snorted at his own joke and realized he was improbably happy again. He'd been tapping the wheel and humming under his breath without being aware of it. Go figure.

The sunshine that streamed into the truck was warm enough that he cracked a window. He didn't dare take off his leather jacket in case he had to run. The weather had changed in the past few weeks. What had been hot and humid was now cool, and the trees were beginning to show their autumn colors. The drive should have been another 120 miles, but it was probably over 150 with the back roads. He was good on gas, even if he had to backtrack a few times.

He was riding along one of the larger roads toward Northfield, allowing himself the vision of being at Kingdom Come by nightfall, when he hit a wall. And it wasn't a figurative wall. It was a cinderblock, brick and stone wall built just north of a two-road intersection. It met a large building on one side and a house on the other before resuming in the distance.

He pulled parallel to the wall and climbed to the roof of the pickup. The buildings of a small college sat on the left, residential houses to the right. The white buildings of the college were surrounded by trees just turning gold and orange. It was a pleasant, albeit deserted, scene. There wasn't a living creature behind the wall, although an overturned thermos and a grouping of chairs made it look as though someone had defended it at some point. "Hello? Anyone here?"

There was movement across the parking lot. A Lexer appeared, followed by a dozen more. He knew they didn't sleep when they weren't actively chasing people, but once they caught wind of you it was like they woke up. Peter was in the truck and southbound before they got close. It was back to the small roads and possible logjams for him.

***

It all went wrong on Route 100. He'd had no choice but to take it; the twisting roads all deposited him on the main road for at least a few miles, and he had to pass under I-89. He was weaving his way through a maze of cars on the bridge that led to the overpass, when there was the pop of a gunshot and the front tire blew. His first thought was *duck*, and his second was *fuck*, and then the pickup veered left and came to rest on one of the cars that suddenly didn't seem so randomly spaced. He'd been following a maze, all right, one that had been designed to slow a car down and give the people who'd created it plenty of time to take a shot. His head smacked the steering wheel, but he'd been going slow enough that he was fine.

"Get out of the truck!" a man's voice called from under the overpass. "Now!"

Peter moved the driver's seat back so he'd have more room to crouch while he swung open the door. "What do you want?" he yelled. It was hard to get his voice to carry; his mouth was a desert.

"I want you out of the truck!"

He held his pistol and debated what to do. Whatever they wanted, it wasn't going to end well. They could have everything he had, which wasn't much, but anyone who had put this much thought into staking out travelers probably wasn't letting them go.

He called again to pinpoint the direction of the voice. "Why?"

The windshield cracked with the force of another bullet, and the voice came again. "Get out of the truck or we'll shoot until you *can't* get out."

The speaker was a hundred feet ahead, behind one of the concrete pillars. Peter reached to the passenger seat and grabbed his pack, then shoved the map in and slung it over one shoulder. He put his pistol in the crack of his open door and fired at the pillar. He waited as several shots were returned. They came in order—boom, boom, boom—like there was one shooter, not several. Maybe they didn't want to waste ammo, but Peter thought there should have been more action than that one lone voice and gun. It seemed like someone desperate, which could go either way. Either they were desperate enough to let him go if he gave them his supplies, or so desperate they'd kill him on sight.

"I don't have much," Peter called. He had to work hard at it, but he managed to sound unafraid. "But it's yours if you let me walk away. I just want to get north."

There was a full minute of silence from the pillar. Then a bullet hit the door. He guessed that was his answer. It pissed him off. You could offer someone the shirt off your back and they would still kill you. So be it. He fired at the pillar again, waited for the answering shots, then again, more shots, and then there was a pause. Maybe they were reloading, or rethinking, but this was his chance. He pulled the keys out of the ignition—they'd have a tough time moving the truck without them—threw them off the bridge and ran around the back of the pickup. There was another road to the northwest that he could take under I-89. He lowered the tailgate and pulled the bike to the ground.

He'd stay low and run the bike back through the maze of cars. The road turned at the end of the bridge, and he'd be long gone before they moved the truck and came after him. They might not even bother. He leaned out and fired again. This time there was no answering fire, but he heard soft thuds, like sneakers on concrete. They came again in a quick patter and then stopped, similar to the racing of his heart.

He made sure his feet were behind the pickup's tire and peered beneath the truck. The noise came again, along with the clink of metal. Then, two cars ahead to his left, he saw the tip of a sneaker come out from behind a car. There was a soft swishing noise and the foot extended into the road, as if its owner had slid to the ground. The ragged bottom of a denim-clad leg came into view.

Peter knew he was soft-hearted, but he didn't want to kill living people if he didn't have to. There were so few of them left. But he would. He lay down on the road behind the tire and lined up his sights on the fleshiest part of the man's calf. He exhaled partway, just as John had taught him, and pulled the trigger.

The explosion of denim and blood surprised Peter with its brutality. He'd pictured more of a puncture wound, like Nel had gotten, although that'd been near the edge of the meaty part of his calf. This .45 round had destroyed the man's shin. He was zombie bait now. Peter found he didn't care; his heart could be as hard as anyone's.

He reached for his bike but ducked when he heard footsteps between the agonized shrieks of the man he'd shot. Maybe there *was* more than one person under the overpass. But these footsteps weren't racing to help their comrade, and they weren't stealthy. They came from both ends of the bridge. The noise must have drawn Lexers.

He stayed low, one hand gripping the bike frame, and waited. The footsteps on his side were closing in. They would have to walk past him to reach the cries of pain that had turned to grunts. The man was trying to stay quiet, but Peter imagined it was hard when your leg was almost blown off below the calf.

Hiding was the only option. Peter didn't know how many were coming and whether he'd be able to fight his way through. He slid under the truck, holding his backpack by the hand, and watched the Lexers approach. There were at least a dozen pairs of feet. Sneakers, bare feet with filthy, sore-covered toes and a lone men's dress shoe walked past, intent on the man they could hear and smell.

Peter reached into his pocket and fumbled with the bullets he'd put there, just in case. He fed them into his pistol, silently clicked the cylinder closed and watched as more Lexers followed the first. They fed by the rear of the truck, several tripping on the frame of his bike. The man began to make frightened animal noises. Peter spun so he could swivel his head in either direction. He could only see the back of the man's legs as he pulled himself to his feet—or foot—and leaned on the cars to hop back the way he'd come. The hopping stopped, a few shots rang out, and two Lexers fell to the concrete. But Peter could see more feet coming, just like on his end of the bridge. The Lexers gained on the man. Four more shots came, and then he guessed the man was out because the hopping became wild and desperate. There was a high-pitched scream, so unlike the voice that had demanded Peter leave his truck.

The man hit the ground, and Peter got a glimpse of his would-be assailant. Dark hair, thin face. A regular guy, maybe even a kind person. He dragged himself in Peter's direction, mouth open, until a Lexer landed on him, and he howled as the teeth bit into his back. He caught sight of Peter under the truck, and his eyes went wide. "Help! Help me!"

It was too late to help, but Peter wouldn't have anyway. Some things were worth dying for, but this man who'd thought Peter's life was worth less than nothing wasn't one of them.

Still, it was terrible to watch. They ate him alive, ripped him apart limb by limb, until one knelt by his head and blocked Peter's view. Most of the Lexers passing him had reached the man. Now was his chance. He readied himself to run, but more feet rounded a car behind him. Maybe it was best to wait until they'd moved on. He could stay under the truck as long as he had to.

And, with that thought, the universe decided to mess with him. A Lexer's foot tangled in the bike frame, and it fell to the ground. Peter froze, but the black-rimmed, jaundiced eyes saw him. Its mouth opened, exposing chipped teeth, and it let out a moan that made the others stop in mid-stumble.

There were no more screams from the man to cover this Lexer's hisses, only the wet, quiet sounds of eating. The Lexer tried to drag himself toward Peter, but his feet were caught in the frame. Two Lexers fell to their bellies, and their faces, as pitted and rotted as the first, peered under the truck's chassis.

He had to run. He rolled into the v-shaped space between the pickup and the sedan he'd crashed into. The bike was a lost cause, but he clipped his pack firmly on his back. The sun half-blinded him, and he held his gun aloft until he could see. There were more than a dozen Lexers between him and the end of the bridge, all traveling along the space he'd driven through. He jumped onto the sedan, and then ran up the roof and down the trunk before he leapt to the next vehicle.

Peter was three cars down before the ones eating noticed him. The maze that had gotten him into this mess was the only thing saving him now. He jumped from car to car, and then stood on the hood of a Taurus at the end of the maze, where a group of six Lexers waited. Head shots weren't easy on moving targets, especially ones that moved so randomly, and only when they closed in did he hit three. A glance behind him confirmed about fifteen more would be there in minutes, so he moved his pistol to his left hand, pulled his machete with his right, and jumped into the three standing before him.

The initial leap knocked one to the ground. He jammed his gun left-handed under of the chin of the one who'd grabbed his arm and sent brown gore rocketing into the air. A push on the other Lexer's chest gave him enough clearance to drive the machete blade into its mouth.

He tried to run but was dragged backward by the one he'd knocked to the ground, who'd snuck an arm through his backpack's lower strap and now hung on, teeth snapping. Peter kicked like a horse, but this one wasn't letting go. It was dead weight—dead weight with teeth. The other Lexers were twenty feet away; he was losing his head start.

Peter unclasped the chest and waist straps in order to drop his pack. He might be okay without his supplies, although the odds got slimmer as he lost one thing after another on his way north. But all the supplies in the world wouldn't do him any good if he were dead. In a last ditch effort, he gripped his machete, spun to swing the Lexer out to his side, and then brought the machete down and back in an arc. There was a crunch, the dead weight got even deader, and its grip loosened enough to yank away. The fingertips of the first of the approaching group of Lexers, covered in dried, crackled blood, grazed his arm. Peter barreled to the end of the bridge and ran west on the two-lane road. He was sweaty and terrified, but alive. Alive.

After more than a mile, Peter stopped in the middle of the road and gulped water. His ankle felt okay, which made him thankful to have heeded Rich's advice. He pushed his dripping hair off his forehead and walked to a nearby house. It had an SUV out front and a two-car garage that could have a bike inside. It might be too much to hope that the SUV would start. When he and John had gotten the van that they'd used to leave the cabin, the battery had been so dead that even with a jumpstart the engine would only click. It had taken a new battery to get it going. After five months it was likely a lot of car batteries were dead. He would have tried anyway, except for the problem of having nothing with which to jumpstart. Still, he'd look for the keys and hope for the best.

He cracked a window on the side door of the garage with the hilt of his machete and turned the lock. There wasn't a bike, but there was an ATV. A useless one, he found out, when he tried the key. A quad would've been perfect. Sometimes it was maddening to be surrounded by so many items that could save your life, if only they would just goddamn work.

The connecting door into the house was unlocked, and it was still and quiet inside. Random items of clothing lay on the floor and a small cooler sat by the entrance to the country kitchen. Whoever had been here, a family by the looks of the pictures, had left in a hurry. Peter was down to the last of his water. The fridge was empty, so he checked the cooler.

The stench under the lid was horrendous. The lack of oxygen hadn't allowed for the decayed food to dry out, but it hadn't stopped it from liquefying into mush that smelled like rotten teeth and death. It smelled like Lexers. There were a couple of cans of Pepsi on top of the cesspool of lunchmeat and fruit. He grabbed one, flipped it open, and took a swallow. The fizzy sweetness cut through the sour taste in his mouth. It might have been the best beverage he'd ever tasted. He wanted to savor it, but he was down to the last dribble before he took another breath. Nel would've killed for a can; he'd finished the last of the Pepsi in the nearby Wal-Mart and then gone into withdrawal, like James had from his dearly loved nicotine.

Peter stashed the other can in his bag and took a few packets of soup mix from the cupboards. There was some canned food too, but he left it—he had enough food, and it was heavy. Why hadn't the man under the overpass checked the empty houses? It didn't make any sense. But nothing made sense if you thought by the old rules. Maybe the man had been crazy. Living alone for months would do that to you. Peter sat on the couch, map opened on his lap. He figured he was about sixty to seventy miles away from Kingdom Come. Maybe a two or three days' walk, depending, of course, on what was in his way.

A bike would be faster. He outlined a route in his head and looked at his watch. It was two o'clock. He could get in a few hours, but he'd need to find somewhere to sleep for the night. Also, he hadn't gone that far from the bridge. He didn't know how long the Lexers would follow his trail, but he was running on the assumption that they'd be close to catching up if they walked at one mile per hour.

He left through the front door, tried the unsurprisingly dead truck and jogged up the road. This road would lead him straight through Waterbury and get him past I-89; of course he'd managed to get waylaid in the one part of Vermont that didn't have a thousand dirt roads crisscrossing through it.

He walked as quickly and quietly as possible. At one point, a group of Lexers stood in the road ahead, and he edged through the yards of homes. He could probably outrun them, but he wasn't eager to try that again. Finally, he reached the bridge over the river he'd been paralleling. He considered swimming across the river and walking through the woods until he hit I-89, but without a compass or better map he might get lost. Those were some famous last words right there: *We'll line up the trees and follow them north. It's a straight shot.* No, he was sticking to the road until he was closer.

Peter sighed with relief at the empty bridge. At least something was going right today. He was sure he saw a figure being swept downstream in the river. Zombies couldn't swim, at least. He would've scoured the area for a boat if the river ran north, but the map showed it went west.

Peter crossed onto Main Street and headed toward a house to check for a bike. He'd only come across a couple of kids' bikes so far. He'd laughed at the thought of pedaling through Vermont on the purple Tinkerbell bike in one of the sheds he'd passed, but he damn well would've taken it if it'd fit.

This house looked promising, though. The Subaru out front had a *Share the Road* bumper sticker and a bike rack. He was debating how to get into the garage with the least amount of sound, when he caught sight of a dark mass under the trees in the backyard. He stopped short and held his breath. They hadn't seen him yet. He walked backward, placing one foot lightly behind the other, stopping whenever one looked like it might turn his way.

He was almost out of sight when one did. The growl it let out carried across the road, and it moved his way. He didn't wait to see if the others followed; he was sure they would. He spun on his heel toward the road that branched off Main. It was a dead end—he'd checked earlier—but it was on the right side of the river.

It was a narrow paved road, with houses that might have contained bikes and a gas station store with possible supplies. He ran with the railroad tracks on his left and river on his right, until he spotted a foot trail over the tracks and into the woods. He raced over gravel and through the dark of a pedestrian tunnel, where a Lexer waited, alerted by the pounding of his boots. Peter's eyes adjusted just in time to see its outstretched arms. There was no time to stop, so he slammed it into the wall and kept going, too caught up in his escape to be frightened.

The trail continued into the trees and gradually narrowed until Peter wasn't sure he was still on a trail. Tree branches smacked his face, and he nearly fell face-first onto a boulder in his path. *Calm down.* He forced himself to stop and listen, although his legs shook with the desire for flight. But blindly running into the woods was a stupid idea. He was full of stupid ideas when it came to this kind of stuff. A rich kid raised in New York City didn't have the answers to these kinds of predicaments. Cassie had been raised in the city, but she wasn't rich, and she wasn't your average city kid. She'd still had all her dog-eared and much-loved survival books proudly displayed on her bookshelves when he met her. She'd brought only one out of New York and had given it to the Washington kids. They'd asked her to sign it, like she'd written it herself. He'd found it annoying at the time, but that was because everything had irritated him, including himself. Now, he thought it was sweet. Hank and Corrine had been good kids, like Bits. He hated that all the Washingtons had ever seen of him was a selfish, complaining man who acted more like a kid than the kids did.

It was quiet on the path behind him. Maybe the ones back in Waterbury hadn't seen where he went, and the one in the overpass— which he should have killed but didn't because he was an idiot— didn't seem to have followed. Well, that was good, considering that now he'd lost the path and had no idea which way to go. *Listen for the cars on the highway and follow the sound*, he joked with himself. It was pretty lame, but the fact that he could joke at all showed how Nel and Cassie had rubbed off on him; those two never stopped.

North. As long as he went north, he'd be heading the right way. It was afternoon, so he kept the sun to his left and walked as straight as he could manage. According to his map, as long as he stayed due north and didn't go up any mountains, he'd hit a road eventually. After what felt like just short of forever, he did. He was out of water, and he was saving that second Pepsi, so he filled his bottle at a man-made pond behind a huge, fancy house that boasted a huge, algae-filled pool to match. Whoever lived there had been loaded. He toyed with the idea of entering, but the Lexers, one of whom still had a dusting rag stuck in her apron pocket, rushed the window when they saw him. He strolled away. It used to be that the sight of any Lexer would terrify him, but now he saved his panicking for the ones who could reach him. You had to save your energy and adrenaline to put to good use.

He passed more fancy houses, though none as big as the first. The iodine pills had to dissolve completely before he'd drink his water, and he was counting down the minutes. It would have been nice to have one of the hiking filters, since they worked faster and didn't make the water taste awful like the iodine, but he was glad they'd thought to put the pills in each bag. Shitty-tasting water was better than water that killed you.

They'd gotten sick on their way out of the city because he and Ana hadn't filtered the water. It could have killed them all. Another thing to reminisce about and put in the *Peter was a Jerk Book of Memories*. He was heading for a lively bout of self-flagellation when he realized he had two choices—beat himself up about everything he'd ever done wrong or forgive himself and be who he was now. No one else held a grudge, so why was he doing it for them? He could make this his blank slate. If he made it to Kingdom Come, he would consider himself reborn.

That was all great, but first he had to find his way to a main road because the roads these houses sat on were all loops. They weren't on the map, so he followed one west until he reached one that headed north. Then another, which dead-ended. He needed to get closer to the main road, to roads he could plot on the map, even though it might not be safe.

He came upon a cluster of average homes. He liked these houses better than the big ones. They were more likely to have bikes in their garages and canned food on their shelves, like the house in which he'd spent his first twelve years. His parents had been well-off, but not rich. They'd lived in Westchester, in a nice house with plenty of space and a huge yard, but there'd been bikes in the garage and food on the shelves.

A peeling, green farmhouse had a truck and a sedan out front in spite of the two-car garage. He hoped that meant the garage was full of junk, and that one of those pieces of junk was a bike. He didn't have to break in; the door creaked open and nothing plowed into his machete. There, behind the dusty workbench, stood a men's bike that looked to be a good size. He filled the flat tires with the pump he found and strapped the pump to the back of the bike using one of the many bungee cords that lay in a tangle.

Whoever had lived there had been a slob, but a slob who had almost everything Peter needed. This was his lucky house. Maybe he should try for some more supplies inside. The front doorknob turned easily. Using the tried and true zombie-calling method, he called, "Hello? Anyone here?"

Slow and dragging footsteps sounded. Two Lexers walked across the faded living room carpet. One appeared at the top of the stairs and promptly came tumbling down in its excitement. Peter didn't wait to see it hit the foyer floor. There was nothing he needed badly enough, and by now his water was ready. He gulped a few swallows as the bodies hit the other side of the closed door. No panic, although he did jump. Then he got on the bike and moved on. It was nearing six o'clock, time to find somewhere to sleep. He didn't want to get caught out in the dark.

Peter found it when he neared the main road—a yellow, two-bedroom house that was unlocked. Once he'd verified its lack of occupants, he locked up and lay down on the green couch with his bag beside him. His stomach rumbled, but he couldn't muster the energy to do anything but close his eyes. He kept his holster on and the machete by his side and thought of how he was only forty miles away from Bits, from Ana, even though it felt like a thousand. But, tomorrow, he'd be there. Forty miles on a bike was no problem.

CHAPTER 6

He'd meant to eat but didn't wake until it was almost dawn. The windowless bathroom made for a safe place to use his flashlight to survey his food. Definitely the big packet of slop; he was starving. It said Beef Ravioli, and maybe it was, in an alternate universe. It could have been worse, though; he'd seen the stew and was glad not to have firsthand experience. He swallowed it down and ripped open the packet marked Toaster Pastry. Now that was good. Too bad the whole thing wasn't Pop-Tarts.

He used the dry toilet. It's not like anyone was going to complain, and by the time he'd left the bathroom it was light enough to leave. The kitchen cabinets were empty. That was fine; he had enough food for a few days. What he needed was water; the liter bottle in his pack was pretty low. He grabbed an empty bottle to fill when he next came across water, to replace the one he'd stupidly left in the pickup.

The air was thick with fog, which might help to obscure him from Lexers. It went both ways, though, so he pedaled slowly enough that he could stop if necessary, while still making decent time. The two-lane road passed farmhouses and fields that had grown into wildflower meadows. There was a pileup that looked like it had been moved to allow for a vehicle and assorted Lexers, but the bike made all the difference. He would whiz past, and by the time they'd figured out breakfast had arrived, he was already gone.

The fog burned off and the sky was a clear blue with puffy clouds. A gas station sign loomed ahead. He decided to look for water. Really, any beverage would do. He was almost at the turnoff for the smaller road he planned to take north, and there were probably no stores along it.

The doors to the station's store were locked, which would have necessitated breaking the glass had someone not already done it. It was good he wouldn't have to make noise, but that likely meant it was empty of anything worthwhile. Still, he stepped through the opening and crunched over the glass, past shelves barren of all food, to the coolers that lined the back. Rotten milk and orange juice were the only things on offer. Peter sighed. He'd just guzzled the rest of his water and was still thirsty. He bent down to scan the lower shelves and let out a quiet whoop of joy. There it was, on its side in the back: one small, lonely bottle of water.

He twisted the cap and allowed himself a quarter of the bottle, then stuck it in his pack's side pocket before heading to the door. There was a Lexer sniffing around his bike just outside. It really was sniffing, like a dog. It turned its head in small, jerky movements and grunted at the sight of him. It was almost a greeting. *Hey, how you doing? I'm thinking of eating you.* The machete rasped out of its sheath, and he walked to meet his new buddy halfway. He brought it sideways into the Lexer's neck and pulled it out again.

You had to get the head, but if you got just under the jaw and angled up it did the job with a little less effort. There was enough lower brain there to kill them once and for all, he guessed. He wiped his blade on the grass and threw a leg over the bike. The breeze was nice; it kept him from becoming unbearably hot in all his layers, even with the solid barrier of sweat that had formed between his back and pack.

The turn was just ahead. He was getting closer, and it was morning, with the whole day ahead of him. There was a state park with a lake nine miles north where he'd replenish his water supply. He would've whistled, if he could've done it silently.

Halfway to the state park, he thought he heard noises in the woods. He straddled his bike and stood in the center of the road, straining his ears. A crash came from behind, and he spun around to see Lexers spilling onto the road. Dozens of Lexers. He put his feet to the pedals and picked up speed around the bend, only to find another group. They seemed to be part of the first; he was in the middle of one of those traveling pods Zeke had warned them about. He'd ridden into the calm eye of a Lexer hurricane.

They were too dense to make it through on his bike. He could leave his bike and run into the woods, but it sounded like there were more in there. The breeze wasn't cooling him down any longer. He was a shaky, sweaty bundle of nerves. This was what you saved your adrenaline for. A trailer park ahead on the right, which went by the name *Elmore Estates*, was his only other option. It meant heading toward the limping, growling group coming for him, but he had to try.

He pedaled furiously into the first few Lexers. A set of grimy hands locked on his handlebars, and the bike skittered out from under him. He managed to avoid going down with it and made for the park entrance. Elmore Estates consisted of a loop with park trailers on either side of each lane. The whole place was surrounded by a chain-link fence threaded with green privacy strips. It looked to have been well-kept, but now the flowers in the planters were dead, a few doors hung on their hinges and garbage was scattered throughout.

Peter took the right-hand lane. A trailer with a busted door would be useless, and if he had to bust down the door it would be rendered useless. He ran for the open window of the fourth trailer down on the left and sliced his machete through the screen just as the pod came into eyeshot. They could see him. He followed his bag in and slammed the window down.

He was in an empty living room that had a wide entrance into a kitchen, also empty. The dim hallway had three doors, all closed. That was good enough for him at the moment, so he crouched and moved to the window by which he'd entered. He put a hand on the arm of the floral couch and raised his eyes to the windowsill. He was greeted by yellow teeth filled with black gunk and lidless eyeballs, and he fell back when the Lexer slammed a skeletal hand to the glass. They knew he was inside. They knew, and that meant they wouldn't stop until they were inside, too. As if in answer to that thought, the bottom half of the other window darkened with hands and the front door rattled.

He crawled out of the room, dragging his bag behind him, and then rose to make his way down the hall. The room at the end was his best bet. Maybe he could get out a window and into another trailer. Maybe, through some miracle, he could make it over the fence. Into what, he didn't know, but it had to be better than waiting inside a trailer-shaped coffin to die.

He turned the knob and swung the door open with his machete at the ready. There was a bed with a cheap quilt, and under it lay what looked to be an elderly woman and man. They'd shriveled and shrunk in death, but he could still see the lines etched into their skin from the years they'd been alive. A Ruger Scout rifle—Peter recognized it because John had one—leaned against the bed, a box of ammo beside it. Another gun wouldn't hurt. He shoved the box of ammo in his pack, slung the rifle's strap over his shoulder and moved to the window.

A stretch of overgrown grass ran between the back ends of the trailers. The grass was still clear, but he could see Lexers on the asphalt of the other side of the loop. If he could get into one of the other trailers from the backyard, they could break down this one's door all they wanted. And they were going to; he could hear the wood door splintering from the other end of the house.

He raised the window and shoved out the screen. A quick glance confirmed it was safe to run, and he set his sights on a window two trailers down. There was no reflection behind the screen, which made him think it was open. If it wasn't, and he had to break the glass, he might end up dead. But he was dead if he stayed and dead if he tried for the fence.

His boot hit the sill and then he was out, running in a crouch between the backs of the trailers. The screen tore under his machete. He threw his pack in and followed it to the floor with a thud. He lay there for a moment, trying to hear over his pounding heart, but the sounds of the Lexers didn't draw closer. The window made a squeak that seemed to echo for miles when he closed it. Then he lowered the blind a millimeter at a time. He'd made it. He leaned against the wall and shut his eyes.

They snapped open at the creaking noise down the hall. This trailer was the same layout as the first. He'd entered in the back, into the same end bedroom by which he'd left the other one. His machete lay on the floor; he was so relieved to be safe he'd forgotten that inside could be just as dangerous. Another stupid move brought to you by Peter. Well, he was learning these things the hard way—it seemed to be the way a lesson stuck.

Another creak of floorboards. Better to see what was coming and have a place to retreat than to be trapped in the corner of this bedroom that looked like an eyelet factory had exploded inside it. Peter walked to the doorway. It took a few seconds for his eyes to adjust to the gloom. A little boy, no more than five and dressed in rocket ship pajamas, stumbled down the hall. He wasn't cute any longer, but you could tell he once was by the pudgy cheeks and curly, dark hair that framed his face.

Peter considered pushing him into the room and locking it to avoid having to kill him, but you couldn't be sentimental when it came to zombies. People, even ones like that guy under the bridge, maybe, but not zombies. Peter backed into the bedroom. The boy came into the light, baby teeth grinding and eyes wild. His pajama shirt said *One Giant Leap for Bedtime.* He'd probably loved the shit out of those pajamas. Peter would've when he was a kid.

"Sorry," Peter whispered, and punched the machete into his left eye.

The little guy landed on his side like he was sleeping, one hand up by his face and the other curled over his round tummy. Peter stood over the body for a moment and then closed the bedroom door behind him to check the rest of the house. The boy's bedroom was painted a pale blue and full of toys, with the name *Jonah* spelled out in wooden letters on the wall. All the blinds in the kitchen and living room were lowered and the rooms empty. He wondered how Jonah had ended up alone. Had his parents left him for dead, not realizing what he'd become? Had they gone for help, only to be killed themselves? Had they known, but not been able to bring themselves to kill him? Peter could imagine any number of scenarios; he just hoped Jonah hadn't been scared, that he hadn't had to die alone.

He bit down so hard this time he tasted iron, but the pain didn't match the burning in his chest. So many people had died, alone and scared, crying for their parents, their husbands and wives, their children. Like Jane had probably cried as she sat in their parents' car, surrounded by flames. Peter sank into a chair at the kitchen table, laid his head on his arms and let the tears go.

***

Crying hadn't been the best idea. He may have felt better emotionally, but he was thirstier than ever. His small bottle of water was two-thirds full and an exhaustive search of the kitchen turned up nothing except Kool-Aid mix, peanut butter and some boxes of crackers. Big fucking whoop, he already had crackers. Salty, thirst-inducing crackers.

He peeked out the blinds and saw the park was full of Lexers. They must have broken through the first trailer and found nothing, and now they all stood or wandered aimlessly. One had his arm up on the side of a trailer, head lowered, like he was talking to a pretty girl at a party. Peter walked the house and examined every possible exit, but there wasn't a single spot where there weren't at least a few. It was likely he'd never make it to the far-off fence without a lot of trouble.

The sip of water he allowed himself was delectable. He swished it around his dry mouth and swallowed. He'd wait them out. Surely they'd get distracted and amble off at some point; the pods seemed to like to move. He hoped it'd be before he was too thirsty. How long could you live without water? Two, three days? Longer, maybe, but he felt sure you weren't going to be able to outrun Lexers when you were weakened from thirst.

He sat on the living room's leather couch. There were a few pictures of a family, with Jonah taking center stage. There had been a mom and dad, but obviously Mom had been in control of decorating. The living room was filled with prints of flowers in vases, accentuated by actual fake flowers in vases on both side tables, the coffee table, and the gold and wood entertainment center.

He had to pee and was on his way to the bathroom when he realized he should probably save it. He poked around and came up with a Tupperware pitcher. It was clear plastic, and when he was done he looked at the yellow liquid inside with an unsettled stomach. He couldn't imagine being thirsty enough to drink that. But you never knew how desperate you could get until you were there. Maybe he could add the Kool-Aid to it—he shook his head. He'd figure out how to do it when—and *if*—he had to, but he still had water and the other MRE, which might contain something that was liquid. He opened the outer packaging to reveal packets of beef brisket, biscuit, cookies, crackers and butter granules, among other items. They couldn't have made a drier MRE if they'd tried. The universe was at it again. He hadn't gone far today, but he was tired, so he grabbed the afghan off the back of the couch, rolled to his side and went to sleep.

It was afternoon when he woke. He was still thirsty. Imagine that. He peed into the pitcher again, which already smelled terrible, and sipped at his water. The Lexers were still there. A way to distract them would be great. He went to the back, purposely not looking at Jonah, but there was no way to raise a window and throw something into the distance without being noticed. There went that plan.

The bookshelf in the living room was full of romance novels. Either Dad had liked romance novels too, or he'd not been big on reading. Peter chose one that didn't involve an heiress and sat down to read until dark. When the light through the blinds became too dim, he threw the book aside. His apocalyptic reading material had become bizarre. No wonder Cassie insisted on carrying her own books around; it was probably one of those survival strategies only she and John knew.

He lay back and closed his eyes, but all he could think about was the couple in the book. They'd met at a party, fallen instantly in love and had a whirlwind romance. The girl found out she was pregnant and didn't tell the guy because it would ruin his bright future to be a father at twenty-four. So she raised the kid in some far-off town while he spent almost two years looking for her. Of course, instead of being happy when he found her—since all she'd done was dream of him and stare into the eyes of their son, which were *so much like his father's*—she'd slammed the door in his face. It was maddening. It's not like Peter had been the master of healthy relationships, but *come on*.

Why the hell was he giving this so much thought? Maybe the thirst was already addling his brain. He allowed himself another swig and closed his eyes again. This time he thought of what he'd do when he saw Ana—as long as she didn't slam the door in his face, like some fictional characters he could mention—and the look on Nel's face when he handed him that can of Pepsi he was saving.

Peter sat up and shook his head. How could he have forgotten about the Pepsi? He pulled it from where he'd buried it in the pack and placed it on the coffee table. He could see it shining in the dark, and it was beautiful. Too beautiful to leave on the table. He nestled it on his chest and fell asleep.

The next morning was the same: Lexers outside, pee in the pitcher, eat some crackers with cheese spread, sip water. At least the couple in the book had finally gotten together. He started on another one and rolled his eyes as the series of misunderstandings began. But he could see why people read them—you knew they'd end all right. You couldn't promise that in the real world, certainly not in this world. You could hope it would be all right, you could believe it'd be all right, but you couldn't guarantee it. But Peter decided to believe it. He still had the Pepsi, a few ounces of water and all the crackers one guy could eat.

The characters in the book were constantly drinking, and he began to suspect the author was trying to torment him. Wine, soda, glasses of ice water—they were all there for the taking. They didn't even appreciate it. He rested the book on his lap and stared at the Pepsi. He would open it and take a sip, then transfer it to a container where it wouldn't evaporate.

Peter cracked the top and took two swallows. "Enough," he said aloud, and forced himself to stop. Was it better to drink it all and then go without or slowly die of thirst while sipping? He decided on the latter. At least this way, sip by sip, his body might use it, instead of adding to his pee collection. He hoped the caffeine and sugar wouldn't make his thirst worse.

The Lexers still hadn't moved by late afternoon and his third romance. By nightfall he was so thirsty he allowed himself to finish the water along with the beef brisket. It wasn't winning any culinary awards, but it was much more liquid than he had imagined. That left most of a can of Pepsi and his third day of captivity to look forward to tomorrow.

Another day, another romance. By noon Peter could think of almost nothing but beverages. He'd even drink prune juice, his nemesis, gladly. A couple of sips of Pepsi at one o'clock made him so thirsty that he allowed himself to dip his tongue into the container a few hours later. He was tired, more tired than a person who sat around reading romance novels all day should be, and when darkness fell so did his eyelids.

The next morning his mouth was glued shut. He eyed the five remaining ounces of Pepsi on the counter next to the many ounces of piss. He could almost see how that would be appealing, when the Pepsi was gone. Well, not appealing, but better than nothing.

Two ounces in the morning, one in the afternoon, one in the evening and one for tomorrow. It was amazing he could even pee into the pitcher still. Where was his body getting the liquid? Why wasn't it using it? He wanted to punch his bladder, but instead he read his book in between naps, and then fell asleep for the night.

Day five's ounce of Pepsi was bittersweet. That was it. He ignored the pitcher on the counter and ate the packet of barbecue sauce that was in the MRE. It moistened his mouth, but the salt was probably going to make it worse. He sucked on a mint from his beef ravioli MRE and stared at the ceiling. He didn't know if it was his imagination or he really was weak and tired. He had no energy. Whether that was because he was dehydrated or because the Lexers outside were going to outlast him, he didn't know.

They were going to win.

The thought made him sit up. No, they weren't going to win. Fuck them. He was going to see Bits again. If they were still there tomorrow he'd drink some Kool-Aid pee and run. It would be all right. He lay back down and drifted into a sleep filled with dreams of running faucets and coolers full of ice cold beverages.

He woke up at dawn thinking about hot water heaters. If it had been a dream, he couldn't remember it. His brain was fuzzy and begged for a few more minutes of rest. No sense in rushing into what was next on the menu; might as well rest for the big event.

Hot water heaters.

Peter jumped off the couch so fast that the large coffee table vase crashed and broke. He cursed and peeked through the blinds. At least the Lexers hadn't heard.

Cassie and John often had enthusiastic discussions about random survival tactics. Heating rocks in a fire and burying them under a thin layer of dirt in a makeshift shelter to stay warm, starting fires without matches, that kind of thing. They were both kind of crazy, if you thought about it. But he recalled a conversation about hot water heaters. Even after the main water ran dry, the water in the heater's tank remained. Every house had gallons of potable water there for the taking. He moved down the hall on unsteady feet and found the tank in the closet that held the stackable washer and dryer. It wasn't huge, but thirty gallons was a lot of water. He could outlast the Lexers with thirty gallons.

There was the spigot on the bottom; now he needed a bowl from the kitchen. The hand that held the bowl shook as he turned the spigot and waited for that rush of cool, life-sustaining water. A trickle ran into the bowl and stopped. Peter drank the water before he did something ridiculous like spill it. It was so good that he groaned, but it was a tease. That couldn't be all there was. If he hadn't wanted to conserve every ounce of liquid in his body he would have cried in frustration. There should be water in there.

Then he remembered—it was a vacuum. Sometimes you had to open a faucet or valve so the water would drain. He closed the spigot, turned the bathroom tap on, sat with his bowl at the ready, and turned the knob. Nothing. Now he was getting pissed. There was water in there, and it was his, damn it. He'd hack open the top if he had to.

But he started with busting the hot water pipe on the top, since he couldn't find some valve he thought John had mentioned. He said a silent prayer, turned the spigot and exhaled at the solid stream of water that flowed into the bowl. It wasn't the cleanest-looking water on Earth, with tiny grains of sediment that settled in the bottom, but it wasn't pee, and that was good enough for him. He guzzled the bowl and went for a refill. God, it was amazing stuff, that water. Later he'd drain part of the tank into containers to see how much he had in total, but for now all he wanted was another bowl. He'd known it would be all right. And he would never, ever make fun of Cassie and John again.

By nightfall, he thought he saw fewer Lexers outside but couldn't see far enough into the darkness to be sure. He readied his pack, just in case he could leave in the morning, and stuck the book he was reading inside. He knew it would work out all right, but he still wanted to finish it.

In the morning he made Kool-Aid, something he'd never had as a kid. It was tantamount to poison, according to Mom. He enjoyed every drop of it along with some crackers. There really were fewer Lexers out there. Maybe a couple dozen left, all spread out. He could outrun them, especially if his bike was still on the road outside the entrance.

He tapped his fingers on the kitchen counter and mixed up more Kool-Aid. He had to leave soon. It was almost a week here, which meant it was approaching October. He could get stuck like this again, it could snow, and then he might never make it. Although, if the Lexers froze before he did—and with no heat that was a crapshoot—he'd be able to walk there without worry. This might be his best chance. He made sure his bottles were full, dumped his pee down the kitchen drain, and filled a container with Kool-Aid. It was pretty good stuff, although he'd never feed it to Bits. He'd read the ingredients; Mom was right.

Peter buckled his pack, slung the rifle over his shoulder and held his machete. Then he strode to the door, took a breath and ran onto the asphalt. He shoved one who got too close, dodged the others and pounded past the homes he'd passed on the way in. The bike lay on its side where he'd left it. He glanced behind him to be sure he had time and bent for the handlebars. He ran alongside it, swerving around the few Lexers in the road, before jumping on and pedaling like a madman, widening the gap with every rotation. The mirror on the handlebars had twisted when the bike fell, but now he straightened it out in time to see the Lexers from the park reach the road.

"So long, lollipops," he called. Then he turned his gaze north and didn't look back.

By noon he was less than ten miles away. There had been more than a few pit stops due to all the water and Kool-Aid, but he'd made good time. The thirty miles he'd biked had been a cakewalk in comparison to the rest of his journey, since he'd only run into a few Lexers here and there, but his thighs burned from the long, relentless hills. The cars had been pushed aside in a few places, and now, so close to the farm, the roads were completely clear. He hoped that everyone had come the same way, that the pickup had gotten them there.

Just outside the tiny town before the farm, his bike tire blew with a loud pop. Peter used his feet to swerve to a stop, narrowly avoiding a nasty fall, and looked at the clouds that floated in the sky.

"Really?" he asked them.

The tube was torn beyond repair, not that he had a repair kit anyway. He tried riding on the busted wheel, but he could walk faster. His backpack wasn't too unwieldy when he was going fast, but he looked like Cassie learning how to ride a bike with all the wobbling he did riding on the wheel's rim. He smiled at the mental image. She was such a dork; who couldn't ride a bike? But she could, now that he and Bits had taught her.

Cassie had gained some grace this summer, though, like she'd finally gotten the hang of bike riding. She still managed to step on someone's toes or spill something at least once a week—that would never change—but she could fight. Her eyes glowed light green when there was a threat, and the set of her mouth left no doubt that she'd kill if she had to. Maybe it was shooting Neil that had changed her, along with Ana's constant nagging for a sparring partner. When you watched her and Ana practice together, Ana's dark, gold-flecked eyes even deadlier than Cassie's, you were very glad to be on their side.

Picturing the two of them made Peter more confident that they were safe. They would kill anything in their way, alive or dead. He put his boots to the concrete and walked. The road was clear, the sun was bright, and the trees were more colorful than in southern Vermont. The weeds that should have been fields of corn or wheat or whatever they grew up here were turning brown. A flock of geese flew overhead in a messy V. It was a gorgeous fall day, the kind that people used to pay a good bit of money to visit.

At the outskirts of the tiny town, he kept as close to the shadows as he dared. He didn't want to draw the attention of the Lexers that were surely lurking. But he was astounded to find the village green empty. It was like a ghost town, in a good way. The general store up ahead had a sign out front that offered gas and food inside, as well as lodging at Kingdom Come. He continued up dirt roads and past a farmhouse with a serious-looking fence, and then took a left onto Kingdom Road. He'd listened to the directions so many times on the radio that he could recite them verbatim.

There was a cabin up on legs at the side of the road. A guy, no more than twenty, sporting a platinum ponytail and rifle, came down to greet him. "Hey, I'm Caleb."

He shook the kid's hand. "Peter."

"You coming to stay?"

"I think so." Peter glanced up at the woman with short, dark hair who stood on the cabin's platform, leveling a rifle at his head. Her mouth twitched in greeting at his smile. "It was a long trip."

"It looks it, man," Caleb said with a laugh.

The jeans Peter had washed at Chuck's for his one-day drive had been clean. Now they were brown, and the button-down under his coat wasn't in much better shape.

"You want a ride to the gate?" Caleb asked, and pointed at a pickup. "It's about a quarter mile."

Two minutes later, Caleb left him at the metal gate with a guy named Dan, who let him in a side door. Dan shook his hand and introduced him to a woman and a man who sat at a folding table. Peter was so preoccupied with his next question that he didn't catch their names.

"We usually have a truck down here," Dan said, "but they drove it up today. I'll walk you if you want. It's not far."

Peter nodded. They all looked so tranquil, but he couldn't relax until he knew. He pulled off his jacket and threaded it through a strap of his pack, sweating more than he had during the bike ride. "Did someone named Cassie Forrest come here with a group of people? They know Adrian."

The creases around Dan's eyes deepened when he grinned. "Sure, they got here maybe a month ago. With Bits and the others. You know them?"

Bits was here. Peter felt so light he could've sworn his boots had left the ground. Everything grew blurry, but this time he didn't bite his cheek to stop the tears. Bits was here. He didn't ask who the others were, just in case Dan left someone out by accident. He was afraid to ask about Ana. If it was bad, he wanted Cassie to be the one to tell him.

"Yeah," Peter said. He wiped his eyes. Dan looked so pleased for him that it was impossible not to smile back. Reunions were rare these days. "I know them."

"Call Cass on the radio," Dan said to the guy at the table. Then he put a hand on Peter's shoulder and motioned up the road.

Dan said something. Peter nodded along, but he wasn't listening. He was watching the gold and red leaves float to the dirt road and praying they were all there. Then he heard something besides Dan's friendly voice—the sound of bare feet slapping the ground. He only knew one person who ran around barefoot as much as she could.

Peter looked up as Cassie rounded the bend. She stopped— mouth open, eyes wide—almost like she hadn't been sure it was him she was going to find.

"Peter!" she called, and ran toward him.

Her laugh was so carefree and her smile so wide that he was almost positive they'd all made it. But, no matter what, he still had a daughter and a best friend. He still had a family. He was home.

ABOUT THE AUTHOR

Sarah Lyons Fleming is a wannabe prepper and a lover of anything pre-apocalyptic, apocalyptic, and post-apocalyptic. Add in some romance and humor, and she's in heaven.

Besides an unhealthy obsession with home-canned food and Bug Out Bag equipment, she loves books, making artsy stuff and laughing her arse off. Born and raised in Brooklyn, NY, she now lives in Oregon with her family and, in her opinion, not nearly enough supplies for the zombie apocalypse. But she's working on it.

Visit the author at www.SarahLyonsFleming.com

Other books by Sarah Lyons Fleming:

The *Until the End of the World* series
Until the End of the World (Book one)
So Long, Lollipops (Peter's Novella, Book 1.5)
And After (Book two)
All the Stars in the Sky (Book three)

The City Series
Mordacious (Book one)
Peripeteia (Book two)
Instauration (Book three)

The Cascadia Series
World Departed (Book one)
World Between (Book two, coming in 2021)
World Undone (Book three, coming in 2022)
World Anew (Book four, coming in 2023)

ACKNOWLEDGEMENTS

I'm gonna keep this short and sweet—you know, 'cause it's a novella. Thanks to my parents, who always read and then read again. Recently, I was surprised to find that many writers' families don't read their work. I already knew I was lucky, but man, I must've hit the jackpot!

To my lovely friends/beta readers, who drop all other books to read mine. Thank you Allie, Danielle, and Jamie!

Tons of love and appreciation to my husband, Will, who reads with a keen eye and an understanding of the craft of writing that I'll never have, and who forces me to dig deeper and then come up with the words to describe what I've unearthed.

Made in the USA
Las Vegas, NV
16 November 2024

11945835R00046